HL-11

114906

$15.95

LPB
RAIN   Raine, William
         MacLeod,
              High Grass Valley

JAN 1 9 1995

114906

MLW

AP 91

HIGH GRASS VALLEY

*Also by William MacLeod Raine
in Thorndike Large Print*

Glory Hole
Under Northern Stars
The Fighting Edge

HIGH GRASS VALLEY

By William MacLeod Raine

Thorndike Press • Thorndike, Maine

Library of Congress Cataloging in Publication Data:

Raine, William MacLeod, 1871-1954.
  High Grass Valley / William MacLeod Raine.
    p. cm.
  ISBN 1-56054-108-3 (alk. paper : lg. print)
  1. Large type books. I. Title.
[PS3535.A385H54   1991]   90-25147
813'.52—dc20   CIP

Thorndike Press Large Print edition published in 1991
by arrangement with Patricia R. Barker.

Cover design by James B. Murray.

The tree indicium is a trademark of Thorndike Press.

This book is printed on acid-free, high opacity paper. ∞

Foreword

William MacLeod Raine died July 25, 1954. His passing marked the end of an era, for he was the one working writer of Western fiction whose career reached back to the days when the events about which we write actually took place. In point of time, Owen Wister and Stewart Edward White were ahead of him, but as far as I know, the dozens, I suppose we could say hundreds, of authors who made and are making a living writing Western fiction came after him.

Shortly before his death *Time* published an article about Mr. Raine which quoted a beginning writer as saying, "After all, he was here when the guns went off." That is literally true, for he knew many famous men who had a big part in shaping the West, names such as Bat Masterson, Jeff Milton, Bill Tilghman, Burt Mossman and Pat Garrett. He rode with these men, ate with them, sat by campfires at night and talked to them. As correspondent at various times for magazines and newspapers, he traveled all over the West covering such exciting events as the Tonto Basin feud, the Montana copper war, the hunt for Harry Tracy the escaped convict, and the activities of the Arizona Rangers. This was the background upon which he drew when he wrote his Western fiction, and it explains, I think, the ring of authenticity which is consistently found in his work.

When I began writing nearly twenty years ago, William MacLeod Raine was more than a writer. He was a legend. When I moved to Colorado several years ago, I had the privilege of meeting him personally. That made the move worthwhile, if nothing else did. Bill Raine was the kind of man who, once known, could never be forgotten. He was always humble, always generous in his appraisal of other writers' work, always willing to talk shop with the beginner as well as the established author.

He was an active member of the Colorado Authors' League and Western Writers of America, and in spite of his years and failing health, he did a great deal for both organizations, even to giving the address at the Awards Banquet at the first annual convention of the Western Writers of America. This was only two months before his death.

He continued to work right up to his final illness, but he was not given enough time to finish *High Grass Valley*. He had once told me that if he died leaving an unfinished manuscript, he wanted me to complete it. At the time I was complimented, but I did not take him seriously. At the age of eighty-three, William MacLeod Raine had the appearance and energy of a man of sixty; to me he seemed as ageless and indestructible as the Colorado Rockies. After his death Mrs. Raine asked me to finish *High Grass Valley*. Although the ending is mine, the book is his, and I hope his many readers will enjoy it as they have the many books that preceded it.

Wayne D. Overholser

Boulder, Colorado
January 22, 1955

Chapter One

Tom MacNeill drew up on the ridge that looked down on Tail Holt and shifted his weight in the saddle to ease muscles cramped from long travel. The scatter of houses back of the crooked main street suggested that the town had grown haphazardly without planning. The few brick buildings, all of them new, emphasized by contrast the shabbiness of a place that had lost its self-respect.

As he jogged down the dusty road a large billboard stared at him. Painted on it was one word, JOHNSTOWN. The name Tail Holt was not respectable enough for the colonel, so he had called it after himself to stress the fact that he owned it, lock, stock and barrel. He had to be czar, Tom thought wryly.

MacNeill swung out of the hull and tied at the hitch rack in front of the new brick bank. A moment of doubt as to his wisdom in coming here stirred in him. He made sure the .45 sagging in its holster from his belt lay lightly for a draw. The invitation might be a trap, but he did not think so. It would not be in character for this man to make an open move against him.

He sauntered into the building, hat slightly tiptilted, the picture of one coolly sure of himself. Tom wished it were true.

Colonel Johnston was giving the teller some direction about answering a letter, but at sight of MacNeill he smiled a welcome and came forward to shake hands. He was a handsome man with a head of fine silken hair entirely white. Dressed in the finest broadcloth cut in the latest mode for a prosperous eastern businessman — a Prince Albert coat, striped trousers, custom-made boots highly polished — he made an impressive and benevolent figure. In this frontier town he was the only man who wore a silk hat.

Tom knew that smile was as false as Satan but he accepted the proffered hand. He had come on invitation, presumably to meet a gesture of peace. Though he had no faith in it, he would listen.

There was a fourth man in the room. He sat in the space back of a railing which led to an inner office. His fingers were busy rolling a cigarette but his light blue flinty eyes never shifted from MacNeill. Tom knew this must be Black Dillon, guard of the banker, often called the Shadow because Johnston seldom appeared in public without this man hovering over him. He was powerfully built, with deep broad shoulders and not a spare ounce of flesh on him. The muscles of his thighs, outlined by tight trousers, were packed like ropes of steel. Dillon was a Texan, a notorious gun-slapper. Victims of his skill had been buried in half a dozen border towns.

"Glad you came, Mr. MacNeill," the banker said heartily. He opened the gate and motioned for his visitor to precede him. "In my office we can fix up this little difficulty."

Black Dillon rose and followed them into the small room. No stranger carrying a .45 on his hip was permitted to see the colonel alone.

Tom did not appear to notice the guard but before he seated himself he shifted the chair in front of the desk in order to face both men.

"I'll be frank with you, young man," Johnston said to his visitor. "The location of your claim interferes with the working of my Molly Green. Of course it has only a nuisance value, but it is too close to us. There will be constant disagreements about encroachments on each other's territory."

"There is one already," Tom replied. "Your men are tunneling to hit our lode."

"Now, Mr. MacNeill, they wouldn't do that," Johnston said in bland reproach. "I want only what is right. Yet what you say

11

proves my point. There is room for only one of us. I will make you and your partners a fair offer for the Argonaut."

"Not for sale," Tom told him bluntly. He added, with a straight face, "Perhaps you would like to sell the Molly Green."

"Let us not be humorous, Mr. MacNeill. Neither you nor your partners have any money. You are working on a shoestring with no means to pay the few men you employ. Presently you will have to stop operations. I don't think your title is good, since I was on the ground first, but I will pay a thousand dollars for the claim."

"How do you happen to know so much about our financial position?" Tom asked.

"I make it my business to know," Johnston answered, "and I am in a position to find out things like that."

Tom did not mention that the colonel's source of information was not as accurate as he thought. The Argonaut was already paying more than expenses. He did not want to excite Johnston's greed. In spite of his suavity the man was a dangerous neighbor.

"Make it a hundred thousand and I'll talk it over with my partners," the young man countered. "And since we are being frank, Colonel, let us face the facts. Your Molly Green is a dud. The only pay ore you will ever take out of it will be stolen from a vein that apexes in our property. As for our title, it is perfectly legal. If you don't think so, why not bring suit to dispossess us instead of trying to run us off by dirty means?"

Black Dillon spoke for the first time, a threat in his low voice. "Maybe I had better take care of this, Colonel."

Johnston neither accepted nor rejected the offer. "You are a brash young fool," he said to MacNeill, his eyes hard as obsidian. "Nobody talks to me like that. You had better amend your manners and accept my terms."

"Or Mr. Dillon will do the talking," Tom suggested. He was skating on thin ice and knew it, but unless he was ready to throw up his hands in surrender it would be a mistake to show any weakness.

"You used a word I will not take," Johnston said, anger in his voice. "You spoke of ore stolen from your vein. I demand a retraction."

Tom took time to answer without undue haste. "Let me put it this way, Colonel. If your superintendent continues to follow a drift he is working now it will soon be in our territory," he said pleasantly. "I have notified Mr. Morse of that."

"I see you are a fool," Johnston said bluntly. "Understand that I don't have blackmailing interlopers adjoining the Molly Green. I give you and your partners two weeks to get out. If you stay, it is at your own risk."

MacNeill rose. "We won't be driven out, Colonel. We sank our shaft in good faith, not to blackmail you for a sale. I'm sorry it has to be this way."

Black Dillon said, with a thin-lipped grin, "You won't be sorry long."

Tom looked at the guard's evil wolfish face and a shudder ran through him. This fellow would snuff out a life with no compunction. He would enjoy doing it.

"I advise you not to be stubborn," Johnston warned. "You may have a long happy life before you — *if you drop your lawless ways.*"

He could not have made his threat plainer. Tom felt as if somebody was walking over his grave. He backed to the door, opened it, and walked out of the bank. Swinging to the saddle, he rode up the street. The sun was shining warmly on a scene peaceful as a New England Sabbath but the sense of doom hung heavily over him.

That this was Johnston's town was accepted sullenly by its inhabitants. Nobody who openly opposed him could long remain and do business here. He owned the bank, the big Johnston Mercantile Emporium, and the Wagon Wheel gambling house. Most of the store buildings on Trail Street belonged to him. A score of homes in the place were mortgaged to him. He was the mayor, and no antagonism was tolerated.

To Tom, brought up in the outdoor free West, it seemed a dreadful thing that a district should be held in peonage. The mining center of Three Cedars, where the Molly Green and the Argonaut were located, was twenty-five miles from Tail Holt but the man was reaching out to establish his despotism there too.

The crest of the saw-toothed range toward which Tom was riding lifted to a sky of azure blue. From the valley the road he was following led him into the foothills. A fine rain blotted out the peaks and softened the raw outlines of the slopes to a misty blur. He untied the slicker from the back of the saddle and slipped into it.

As he got deeper into the hill country the trail grew steeper, winding up gulches and along the shoulders of rock-strewn slopes. It brought him through a scatter of stunted pines to a ridge overlooking a saucer-shaped basin on the far side of which was Outlet Pass.

He descended to the valley and rode beside a small stream which tumbled down the canyon that was the gateway to the pass. A gorge cut into the main canyon and down it the brook cascaded in turbulent little water-

15

falls. The last hundred yards below the pass was a stiff climb among the boulders that had crashed from the walls above during the past thousand years.

At the summit he drew up his panting mount to rest and caught the first view of Three Cedars. The small mining camp lay on a ledge of a spur projecting from the main range. In the clear untempered light of the Southwest he could see the shaft houses of the mines plainly though they were several miles away. Rays from the declining sun hit the tin roof of the Molly Green boardinghouse and transfigured the metal to gleaming gold.

A touch of the spur set his pony in motion. Huge boulders flanked the trail. Too late Tom realized that he had ridden into a trap. The loop of a rope snaked out, dropped over his head, tightened and pinned his arms. He was dragged from the saddle and rapped on the head with the barrel of a revolver.

Tom came out of a dizzy world to find himself in the hands of three men. He had been disarmed and one of his captors was fastening a tie rope around his wrist. His first coherent thought was that if they meant to kill him they would not be taking the trouble to make him a prisoner.

"Kindness of Colonel Johnston?" he asked.

"Don't ask questions," a man ordered curtly.

He was the only one of the three that Tom recognized and he was evidently the leader. The man was Dolph Metzger, manager of a big gambling house in Tail Holt called Wagon Wheel, a heavy man, cold-eyed, once hard and muscular but with a body now running to fat.

Tom loosened his bandanna and wiped away the blood on his face. A bandy-legged squat young fellow tied the handkerchief over the wound for a bandage. He wore a cowboy's chaps.

"Much obliged, Doc," Tom said.

"Oh hell," the range rider demurred, slightly embarrassed at his humane gesture. "Had to fix you so you could travel."

"Nick is a plumb fountain of kindness," Metzger jeered.

They hoisted Tom into his saddle and headed down the canyon up which he had just come.

Chapter Two

For a time after his capture Tom MacNeill could do nothing more than stay in the saddle. He rode with his head down, fingers clutching the horn. They moved single file down the canyon, Dolph Metzger leading. The bandy-legged cowboy called Nick rode behind Tom. The third man brought up the rear. Metzger called him Sowder and Nick referred to him as Hank. He was a big sullen man who looked like one of the colonel's ruffians, but Metzger was plainly the leader of the three.

Tom had no idea why they had taken him prisoner. Metzger had not given him any hint. If Johnston thought he could force Tom's partners, Ben Scanlan and James Campbell, to sell the Argonaut by killing Tom, or by holding him prisoner, he didn't know his men. But whatever the plan was, this was typical of the way Colonel Johnston operated.

The rain had stopped, but the clouds hung low over the peaks and the air was cold and damp. Tom's head still hurt, but he wasn't dizzy now and he was able to think straight. They were climbing through timber. This was the Hardscrabble country, a perfect place to hold a prisoner. It had been thoroughly prospected without a single discovery being made. The soil was so thin that even the grass was poor. As far as Tom knew, no one lived here except a few nesters on the ridges to the south.

Tom guessed where they were headed. Up near the summit a French prospector named Rubideau had built a cabin years ago. Tom remembered riding past it last fall with James Campbell. It was still in good condition. At the time Tom hadn't thought anything about it. Now he wondered if Colonel Johnston kept it up, using it over and over for the same purpose he was going to use it today. A man like the colonel would have many occasions to bend someone to his will by methods he could not use in Tail Holt.

The rain started again, harder than before, and within a few minutes the trail was muddy and slick. Metzger glared at the sky, cursing in anger. He said, "I'm going to get wet before I get back to Tail Holt."

The man he called Sowder spoke up for the first time. "There's one way to fix this so we could all go back to town."

"You've had your orders," Metzger said curtly. "See that you remember them."

19

He did not have long to live, Tom thought bleakly. Metzger's job was to run the Wagon Wheel. He wouldn't stay here long. His conscience was stunted, if he had one at all, but he could be depended upon to do what the colonel wanted. Sowder was a killer. Nick wasn't, but Tom doubted that the bandy-legged rider could handle Sowder if it came to a showdown between them.

An hour or so later they reached the cabin that was set on a ledge directly below the summit. Metzger reined up and dismounted. "Get down," he told Tom. "Sowder, take care of the horses. Nick, rustle some wood. It will be dark before I can get back to Tail Holt. I might as well eat supper here."

For a moment Tom thought the cabin was spinning like a top when he stood beside his horse. Metzger said, "Get moving. We have a little business to transact."

Tom walked to the cabin, Metzger two paces behind him. The door was open. Nick had gone in, got an ax, and come out again. Tom went inside. The cabin had the musty smell of a room that had been closed for a long time. There was very little furniture: a home-made whipsawed table, a cookstove, several three-legged stools of the kind used for milking by hill nesters, and some bunks in the corners farthest from the stove.

Metzger pointed to one of the stools. "Sit down." He drew a folded piece of paper from his inside coat pocket. "MacNeill, you are a fool. You know that nobody bucks the colonel in this country. I don't savvy why you went to the bank if you didn't intend to take his offer."

"I don't savvy myself," Tom admitted, "now that I have had time to think about it."

"The colonel allowed that a little treatment might change your mind," Metzger said. "That's why you're here. I have a deed that is ready for your signature. If you will sign it, selling your share of the Argonaut to the colonel, you will be released and you can start for Three Cedars tonight."

Nick came in with an armload of wood and began building a fire. Tom watched him, ignoring Metzger who stood beside him, tapping the deed against the palm of his left hand. Nick looked over his shoulder at Tom. "Go ahead, fellow. Sign it. Me and Hank don't cotton to the idea of staying up here. We can have more fun if we go back to the Wagon Wheel with Metzger."

"Will you sign it?" Metzger demanded impatiently.

"No," Tom said. "It wouldn't do the colonel any good if I did. You will never get Scanlan and Campbell to sell their shares."

"That is his worry," Metzger said. "I have no doubt he knows what he is doing. Our job is to persuade you to sign this deed. If you won't, I will leave you with Sowder and Nick. You will have nothing to eat or drink. You will be tied to the bunk yonder. You will stay in that condition until you do sign. Now I am asking you for the last time. Will you sign?"

"No."

Metzger threw the deed on the table. "You are a bigger fool than I thought. MacNeill, the colonel will wind up owning the Argonaut whether you are alive or not. You will make it easier for all of us if you will sign now and get it over with."

"If I had wanted to sell," Tom said, "I would have done it in Tail Holt when I was in the bank."

"It isn't what you want to do," Metzger snapped. "It's what you are going to do. Why don't you do the only sensible thing —" He shook his head in disgust and turned to the door. Sowder had just come in. "I have changed my mind. I'm going back now. I am afraid you and Nick will be here quite a while."

"I don't figure we will," Sowder said. "Me and Nick will eat beefsteak. When this hombre gets hungry enough after smelling it, he'll come around."

"I think you will be here for a day or two," Metzger said. "Come outside. I want to talk to you."

"There's a shovel in the shed," Sowder growled. "If I dig a grave in one of these arroyos and let MacNeill see it —"

"Just keep the deed handy," Metzger said. "He doesn't want a grave any more than the colonel wants to put him in one."

Metzger stomped out, Sowder following. Nick had the fire going. He stood with his back to the stove, shaking his head at Tom. He said plaintively, "I wish you'd sign that, fellow. I sure hate to see a man starve to death."

"So do I," Tom agreed; "especially when the man is me."

Chapter Three

A horseman topped a rise and from the summit of the small hill watched one of the most memorable sights of cattleland. The Rafter K Bar was busy gathering a beef herd for the market. For weeks the riders had been combing the brush and driving to the roundup all the stock they could find. She stuff and calves were brought along in order that the young could be branded.

It had been a hot day and perspiration poured from the grimy faces of the punchers, sweat from the stained flanks of mustangs. Heat and dust . . . dust and heat. Bawling of fretted cows separated from their offspring, blatting of frightened calves being dragged to the fire where the irons were heating . . . A flanker in striped trousers "going down the rope" to throw the flitter-ear by an upward swing and a pressure of the knees . . . The sizzle of the red-hot iron on the hide of a maverick stretched taut and the acrid smell of burnt flesh . . . Shouts of brown youths on the swing after bolting steers . . . Raucous curse and gay banter . . . Rattle of horns in a milling herd . . . Hi-yi-yippi-yi! From long before daylight till long after dark all hands on the jump. Youth in the saddle and an empire in the making.

The stranger was a miner and he had never witnessed anything like this. He rode up to one of the cowboys fencing the herd.

"Looks like your busy day, son," he said. "I dinna like to bother you, but I must see a lad called Randy MacNeill."

The cowboy lifted his voice in a shout. "Gent to see you, Randy."

A slim lad in chaps cantered across and

joined them. He had been cutting calves out of the herd.

"My name is James Campbell," the stranger explained with a touch of Scottish brogue. "I'm a partner of your brother Tom and I've bad news for you, lad. He is missing."

"Missing?" There was a startled look on the brown well-boned face of the young man.

"He went to Tail Holt to talk with Colonel Johnston. We never saw him again. A man I know in the town, Cal Cotting who runs the Elephant Corral, tells me he was seen to leave there. We can't find anybody who admits to having seen Tom later. I'm more than a wee bit worried, lad."

Fear ran through Randy like a cold wind. "You think Tom has been killed?"

"Maybe not." The miner put a question to him. "Has Tom written you about our trouble with those working the Molly Green?"

"He wrote me that this man Johnston was trying to drive you from your claim."

"Aye, that's what the man wants. He's mad for money and power. In his pay are deevils that would stick at nothing. But he is a canny old scoundrel and might find Tom more useful to him alive than dead."

"How long has Tom been missing?" Randy asked.

"Since Tuesday. I went to Tail Holt and

walked in on Johnston at his bank. Everybody hates the man, so he keeps a gunslinger beside him, a man named Black Dillon. I got just nowhere with Johnston. He can be as smooth as butter. Claimed to be much distressed and sent a search party into the hills to look for Tom. He is as false as Judas. But there was something in his manner — I canna just tell what it was — that made me think he is keeping Tom alive to bargain with. I hope I'm not wrong about that."

"Then we'll have to give him what he wants. Tom's life comes first."

Campbell shook his head doubtfully. He was a man powerfully built, with deep wide shoulders, strong legs slightly bowed, and arms muscled like those of a prizefighter. His face was one to trust. Crowning his head was a shock of red hair.

"It's no' that simple. He'll never admit he has Tom hidden somewhere. But one of his jackals might for him. If we came to an agreement and handed over our mine he might just rub Tom out to make sure he couldn't make trouble later. Then we could prove nothing."

"Then what are we to do?" Randy cried urgently. He was not quite twenty-one years old, tall and lithe but still a little stringy in build. He wore a gray cotton shirt with a blue polka-dot bandanna around his neck. His big floppy hat was old and disreputable.

"You're asking a hard one, son," the miner answered. "It shapes up like this. If Tom is alive, Johnston isn't keeping him at Tail Holt but some place in the hills. Combing the mountain country would be like looking for a lost needle in a haystack. Any information we get must come from Tail Holt, but the hitch is that neither Scanlan nor I can go there to dig it up. We are known men and there would be trouble at once."

"But I could go," Randy said quickly. He tilted his head to look at the sun riding high above them. "If we get a move on us by hard riding we can make tonight's train." He turned to the other cowboy. "Bill, catch up and saddle my sorrel, the one with white stockings, for Mr. Campbell. I'll see the boss and get me Keno from the remuda."

Randy swung his horse and jumped it to a gallop, heading for the man by the fire keeping tally.

"Seems to be a young man in a hurry," Campbell commented. "I like that."

"Randy will do to take along," Bill agreed. "Come with me and I'll get the sorrel for you, Mr. Campbell."

In ten minutes the two men were on their way to the railroad. They started at a road gait. Forty miles had to be covered and it could not be done by foundering the horses. Long before they reached the station Campbell was saddlesore and weary. But he made no complaints. His young companion set the pace and he stayed with it. The approaching train was whistling in the distance when they left their weary mounts at the livery stable and hurried to the depot.

Chapter Four

The young man who turned in his horse at the Elephant Corral was not one likely to draw a second glance at Tail Holt. Many such came in from the range to spend the accumulated wages of long weeks on the sun-baked plains. His red-rimmed eyes looked deeply sunk in their sockets from the untempered glare that beat at them. He wore jean trousers, worn boots, and a checked shirt of blue and white. Tied back of the cantle was a slicker wrapped around a bedroll.

He unsaddled and put his mount into a stall. The horse had been watered at the creek on the edge of town. Before the rider paid any attention to himself he saw that the pony was fed.

The owner of the corral was a spry old man with one leg an inch shorter than the other. His battered Stetson, open vest, and levis climbing up the legs of high-heeled boots announced as plainly as the sun-bleached wrinkled eyes that he had once been a cowboy.

"Aiming to stay long, stranger?" he asked.

"Maybe. Me, I'm tired of chasin' cows' tails. Want to loaf for a spell. After that, well — I don't reckon you know anybody here that needs a hand." He added with a grin that showed perfect white teeth in a brown face, "Name's Lloyd Burns."

"Mine is Cal Cotting," the old-timer answered. "Mostly I'm called Limpy. Busted my leg when I got throwed from a bronc and it never healed good. About a job — I wouldn't know right now. There ain't any saddle jobs in this place."

The man who called himself Lloyd Burns beat the dust from his war sack and opened it. He took out soap and a comb, after which he stripped to the waist and dipped a bucket of water from the horse trough. He scrubbed his face and body thoroughly and sloshed the water over himself to wash away the soap. From the slicker he got a towel to dry himself.

Cotting was a garrulous old fellow who

liked to hunker down on the shady side of a wall and gossip.

"What chance of me getting any kind of job in Johnstown?" Randy asked.

"Name of this town is Tail Holt," the old-timer corrected. "Always has been, always will be as far as I'm concerned."

"Noticed a sign as I came into town. It said Johnstown."

"Call it that if you like," Cotting said huffily. "It's a free country, leastways it used to be."

"Isn't it still?" Randy asked innocently.

Cotting slanted a suspicious look at him but did not reply. But presently he relaxed and answered questions. Colonel Johnston was the big man of the town. He owned the bank, the leading store, the Wagon Wheel, and half the lots on which Tail Holt was built. His right-hand man was Dolph Metzger, manager of the gambling house. Randy noticed that the old fellow was warily careful of what he said. His personal opinions showed not in his words but in his voice and manner. He made no mention of Johnston's killers or of his reaching, ruthless greed. That, the cowboy guessed, was the condition of living in this town. Nobody openly criticized the big boss.

"Looks like I ought to see Colonel Johnston about getting a job," Randy suggested.

"Or Metzger. He does most of the hiring and firing except at Three Cedars where the mine is. Morse is the superintendent there."

An apparently irrelevant bit of gossip deflected Randy's thoughts. "Say, a rancher was telling me a man living here — Mac-something-or-other — got lost in the hills and can't be found. How about it?"

"He didn't live here — came and left the same day."

"Must have been a tenderfoot, I reckon."

"I wouldn't know." Cotting's jaw set. That was a subject he did not intend to discuss with chance strangers.

Randy left his war sack at the corral and sauntered up Trail Street. This was a small cattle town now but a few years earlier it had been a mining camp buzzing with activity. The hill across the creek had been known as Gold Crest. The gray dumps of mines long deserted could still be seen there. When the lode pinched out, its hour of glory had departed. A few shacks on the slope were still used to live in but both the business section and most of the residence quarter were now on this side of the creek.

The houses were built of wood, as were the false-front stores and saloons. The only exceptions were the bank, the Johnston Mercantile Emporium, and the Wagon Wheel.

These were of brick, well constructed and spacious.

For a day or two Randy MacNeill, now Lloyd Burns, did the things characteristic of a cowpuncher on the loose blowing in his wages to see the elephant. He gambled a little, bellied up to the bars, made casual acquaintances. Nobody paid any attention to this gawky range rider so typically verdant and shallow, yet back of his indolence and vacant grin were an urgent impatience and a burning hatred of Johnston and his gunmen. Though haste might be of the utmost importance, he could not afford to show any sign of hurry.

When he mentioned Johnston's name men became guarded. Half of the people either worked for him or owed him money. Beneath his suave surface was a hardness that recognized no rights conflicting with his iron will. In most of those to whom Randy spoke he felt a banked hatred of Johnston's whole group.

Randy had no trouble picking out the colonel's top men. The most prominent were Black Dillon and Dolph Metzger. The manager of the Wagon Wheel was a backslapper full of smiles and apparent good will, but covered by that veneer was a nature callous and cruel. To Randy, who studied them all, the most formidable was the croupier, Calhoun Ives, a slender man with deft fingers and cold black eyes. He was lithe as a cat, graceful, easy and soft spoken, but with the reputation of one as merciless as an Apache in the days when Geronimo was on the warpath, a reputation that had reached as far as the Rafter K Bar range in Colorado.

Chapter Five

The clock in the sky above Tail Holt registered the time as about an hour past high noon. Randy MacNeill was on his way down Trail Street to have another talk with Limpy at the corral. He and Cal Cotting had become friendly and the old-timer was less guarded in his talk. His dislike of Colonel Johnston colored most of his conversation.

A man stepped out of the Cowboy's Rest. His body swayed and he stood outside the batwings with a hand against the wall to steady himself. He had the uncertain look of a man under the influence of liquor. His clothes — the good dark suit, white starched shirt with bow tie slightly askew, and the shining boots — suggested that he was a professional man.

As he started along the sidewalk doubtfully he bumped into Randy. His fingers clutched at the cowboy's coat sleeve and then latched under his forearm. "My friend, if you are going my way I could use your help," he said. "I am somewhat — under the weather."

"I am going your way," Randy answered, pleasantly good-natured.

The stranger introduced himself. "My name is Doctor Edgar. I don't quite recognize you, young man. A visitor here, I think." He spoke with inebriated precision.

"Yes. Lloyd Burns is my name."

"Do your business and get out." There was anger in the doctor's abrupt injunction, a rankling resentment that had nothing to do with Burns. Liquor had loosened his tongue. "If you are a real man you cannot get along here. None of us can. This is a one-man town. He owns us body and soul."

Randy thought that from this chance meeting he might get information.

"One man?" he asked casually.

"Czar Johnston."

"I have heard of him," Burns said dryly.

They left the street and turned into a lane shaded by old cottonwoods. The doctor's silence closed the subject. It had come to him that such talk to a stranger was imprudent.

In front of a small but attractive house Doctor Edgar fumbled with the latch of a gate opening into a garden of old-fashioned flowers. The whole setup suggested a home that had loving care.

Before they reached the porch the door opened. A woman came out, distress pictured on her face. The doctor took off his hat and bowed, apology in his manner.

"A li'l touch of sun, Sallie," he said. "Unfortunate."

The young man just caught her murmured dismay. "Oh, Robert! Again." Burns thought he had never seen a face more sweet or kindly. He knew instinctively that she was a lady, one of few in this raw frontier town.

"Introduce you, my dear, to — to — " The doctor's memory failed to recall the name. He waved a hand at his companion.

"Lloyd Burns," the stranger filled in.

Mrs. Edgar acknowledged the introduction and asked Burns to wait in the parlor for a few minutes until she came down. The doctor stumbled up the stairs, supported by his wife's arm.

The parlor confirmed the visitor's impression that they were nice people. The piano, shelves of books, framed pictures on the wall, the curtained windows spoke of taste. Yet there was no formality. This was a room lived in by a happy family. He had a touch of nostalgia, for he had been brought up by those who knew the comforts of decent habits.

Lloyd Burns, as he now called himself, could not quite make up his mind whether it would be less embarrassing to stay or to slip quietly away. That was something he did not have a chance to decide. He heard the click of the gate latch and from the window saw a young girl racing down the path. Her face was aglow with some happy inner excitement. It had to find vent in action. She threw up her arms and turned a handspring, her long thin sticklike legs upflung from the flying skirts. No puppy wagging its tail with joy could have looked more natural.

Even before she reached the porch she was shouting her good news. "Mother — Mother, I'm getting the Cinderella part in the school play." As she flew into the parlor she sent her straw hat sailing across the room to the top of a table. At the sight of Burns her brown dancing eyes grew big with surprise.

"Good gracious," she exclaimed, and though she did not put the thought into words, he knew she was asking what he was doing here.

He rectified his first impression that she was about thirteen. In spite of the bouncing élan that reminded him of a young colt she must be sixteen or more.

"I brought — I came here with your father," he explained.

Dismay drove all the young eagerness from her face. "Oh dear, is Papa — that way again?"

"The sun was too much for him."

She knew he was lying to cover her humiliation but she accepted his interpretation. It was surprising how quickly the vividness, part tomboy and part elfin, had disappeared to give place to a young woman ready to challenge any criticism of her father.

"It's dreadfully hot today," she said, and her eyes dared him to deny it even in his mind.

Her mother came into the room. She said quietly, "Polly, this is Mr. Burns. I want to talk with him for a few minutes. Would you mind taking the pie out of the oven if it is done?" To the young man she said, after her daughter had gone, "You are a stranger here, are you not, Mr. Burns?"

He replied that he was.

"I thank you for your kindness to my husband," she told him. "Before you leave I want to make an explanation. Doctor Edgar is the finest man I know. He has worked hard here for years, often caring for those from whom he knew he would never receive a penny in return. Of late he has lost a great deal of sleep driving into the country at night to see patients. Yet his fatigue is not the main reason for what you have just seen. This has happened only twice before. He is greatly troubled for fear we shall lose our home. The place is mortgaged and the man who holds the encumbrance is an enemy of Doctor Edgar. My husband fights against evil and speaks his mind freely. One can't do that in this town without reprisal."

"Czar Johnston," Lloyd said grimly.

"You know about conditions here, then?"

"I am learning," he answered.

She looked at this lean lithe youth whose face and bearing seemed not to be in keeping with the poor clothes he wore. There was about him a vigorous strength that might take him into trouble.

"You must be careful what you say here," she warned.

"Is Doctor Edgar careful?" he asked with a boyish grin.

"You are not in my husband's position. Robert is so useful, so popular and so greatly admired, that even Colonel Johnston dare not hurt him physically. All he can do is try to ruin his life." In her voice there was a passionate bitterness.

Lloyd felt a strong admiration for this woman. In her lovely face he saw reflected the qualities that made her a fine wife and mother. The Edgars were the kind of people to whom he was instinctively drawn. But he must put any thought of friendship with them out of his mind. It would not do to involve them in the conflict that was bound to arise between him and the Johnston faction. Yet he might get from Mrs. Edgar proof of a fact he wanted to verify.

"Probably you can't help me," he said. "I came here to find out what happened to a friend of mine who is missing. His name is Tom MacNeill. He is a miner at Three Cedars and he came to town Tuesday on some business — stayed an hour or two and left. He hasn't been seen since."

"I've heard about him," Sallie Edgar responded. "A search party went out looking for him. It's strange he got lost, since he lives at Three Cedars and must have known the country."

"I'm wondering if anybody saw him after he left town. Perhaps somebody from here might have been on the road and met him. If so, he must have passed your house."

"Last Tuesday?" Mrs. Edgar knitted her brow in thought searching her memory. "That was the day I washed. Several people must have gone by on foot." Her eyes lit. "I did see three men riding past as I was taking the clothes in from the line. One of them was

39

Dolph Metzger. The others were strangers. They looked like cowboys."

"Leaving town or returning?" he asked.

"Headed out of town. I don't know how far they went or when they came back. You could ask Mr. Metzger."

"So I could," he agreed grimly. "But I don't think I shall."

She stared at him, startled at the implication of his words. "You don't think — ?" She let the sentence die unfinished.

"Do you know Black Dillon and the gambler, Calhoun Ives?"

"Yes."

"You're sure that neither was with Metzger?"

"Yes, I'm sure," she said. "I would have recognized either of them. And of course Colonel Johnston would never permit Black Dillon to leave him. At least I don't believe he would."

"No, I don't suppose he would," he agreed. "Mrs. Edgar, you will oblige me very much if you do not tell anybody I asked you about this — anybody at all."

His gaze held to hers. In his voice she was aware of a disturbing gravity.

"Of course I won't," she assured him. "But — is it that you think something dreadful has come to him from evil men?"

"I have said too much. It may be that his life and that of others depend on your silence. Will you please be very careful?"

"Yes," she promised. "And you — will you be very wary, too? Dolph Metzger is a dangerous man."

"I won't be here long. But there is one thing I must find out. If Tom MacNeill is alive I must learn where he is being kept. I am afraid I don't have much time, and I dare not ask questions that may stir suspicions."

She trusted this young man as he did her. "Can you come back tonight — after dark? My husband travels the hills a great deal. He made a long ride Tuesday afternoon. It is just possible he might have a guess."

"I'll be here after supper — say nine o'clock."

He left the house with renewed hope in his heart.

When Randy had met Doctor Edgar he had been going to the Elephant Corral. But he changed his mind about that. Just now he did not want to talk with Limpy Cotting, though in the past day or two he had developed a liking for the old cowboy. He wanted to be alone to churn over in his mind the lead that might have opened through meeting the Edgars. He turned from Front Street to the fringe of cottonwoods bordering the creek.

41

Chapter Six

Randy wandered down to the bank of the brawling stream. It was a pleasant spot. The sound of the water rushing down over the stones in the creek was restful and the small whitecaps in the translucent light made a charming picture. He sauntered around a bend in the brook and discovered he was not alone.

A young woman was sitting on a flat stone at the edge of the water. She had taken off her shoes and stockings, pulled up her skirts, and was watching the tumbling waves splash against her shapely legs.

Her mobile face tilted upward at this unwanted trespasser on her solitude. It showed dismay. Young ladies of the period did not expose their lower limbs to those of the opposite sex. But her way of life had taught her not to be prudish. She was in a profession just opening to young women, that of a trained nurse. Moreover, there had been such a flash of shy startled admiration in this young man's eyes that she did not quite want to send him away, since he was plainly more embarrassed than she.

"If you'll turn away and watch the sky for a minute," she suggested, "I'll tell you when."

Vigorously she used the towel she had brought, then drew on her stockings and slipped her feet into the shoes.

"Now, sir," she said.

She had risen to her slim-flanked slender height, a tall girl and a lovely one. A snatch of Whittier jumped to his mind:

> *Our hard, stiff lines of life with her*
> *Are flowing curves of beauty.*

"I'm sorry," Randy said. "I didn't know anybody was here."

She felt sure he had come on her innocently, but thought it a good idea to put him in the wrong. "Maybe you own this creek, sir, and I shouldn't have come here."

"Oh no," he said, and went on to explain, apology in his voice. "This is a nice quiet place where folks don't come much, and I wanted to be alone, so — "

She cut off his sentence. "And I'm interfering with that. I'll take the hint and go at once."

He lifted a protesting hand. "You know I

43

didn't mean for you to go. It's a hot day and this is the coolest spot in town."

A smile he thought enchanting dimpled her cheeks. "You won't be alone if I stay," she reminded him.

Randy was not very sure of himself with young ladies but he understood that he was forgiven. "I've changed my mind about wanting to be alone," he said.

Her eyes danced. "If you will tell me who you want to be with perhaps I can send her here."

He said, surprising himself at his boldness, "She is already here."

She had been appraising him swiftly. He was a cowboy of course fresh from the range. His clothes told her that. But there was something arresting about this young man, not only the lean grace but the steadiness of the gray eyes in his good-looking face. What he wore might be old and soiled but he was young and clean.

"Thank you, kind sir," she said with a little curtsey. "However, since we are strangers I think I had better leave you to your aloneness." Even while she was speaking, a fugitive thought was nudging at her mind that somewhere years ago she had met him.

"But we aren't strangers," he differed. "In a small town we all know one another. You

44

are a nurse from Denver and you have been here about a week visiting the Edgar family who are kin of yours. I don't know your name but that doesn't matter."

"It seems you know something about me, but then I don't know anything about you except that you take short cuts," she told him.

"Not very short cuts. If I am lucky I'll meet you in a few hours."

The girl showed surprise. "What makes you think that?"

"Secret," Randy said. "In case I don't make it I'll arrange to break an arm. Since you are the only nurse in town you would have to nurse me." His grin was meant to let her know that he was speaking in fun.

"You can take another guess. I'm on a holiday." There was a small whiplash in her voice. It was occurring to her that this chance meeting with a strange cowboy had got out of hand and had better be terminated.

Randy watched her go. He would not soon forget the fluent ease of her firm rounded young body in motion.

He was already reproaching himself for having been too brash. Never before had he talked to a young lady like that. What had possessed him to forget himself so impudently? If it was impudence. He had not intended it to be.

Randy went to the Johnston Mercantile Emporium and bought a suit of clothes and a new hat. That evening he did not want to look like a cowpuncher out of a job. He also had his hair cut. In his room he blacked his boots and bathed. For the first time in his life he shaved a second time on the same day. He wanted both Mrs. Edgar and the young nurse to know that he was not an uncouth cow hand.

Mrs. Edgar opened the door at Randy's knock. She took him into the parlor where the family was gathered. The nurse was seated at a table helping Polly work an algebra problem. Her aunt interrupted them.

"This is Mr. Burns," she said in introduction. "My niece, Miss Carlson. You have met my husband and daughter."

If Miss Carlson was surprised at his spruce appearance she did not show it. "I met Mr. Burns down by the creek this afternoon," she mentioned. "But he said he wanted to be alone and of course I left at once not wanting to intrude."

Randy felt himself flushing. "Now, Miss Carlson," he protested. "I didn't mean to drive you away."

The girl turned to her uncle. "Mr. Burns expects to have use for both of us later. He is going to break an arm, then you can set it and

I am to nurse him. Do you think he is a good credit risk?"

Doctor Edgar rose from the armchair where he had been sitting in slippers reading a book. He was laughing as he shook hands with their visitor, but Randy guessed he felt self-conscious on account of what had occurred earlier in the day.

"When and if you break that arm, Mr. Burns, Ingrid and I will both be at your service," he said.

"If I get to riding a jolting bronc on the warpath I may have to take you up on that," Randy replied.

Polly was impressed by this tall long-bodied brown man. "I think Mr. Burns could stick on any horse no matter how much it pitched," she contributed shyly.

Randy nodded thanks but quoted in a cowboy's drawl the old saw:

*"Never was a horse that couldn't be rode
Never was a rider that couldn't be throwed."*

"Have you been a cowboy long?" Mrs. Edgar asked.

"My dad put me on a horse when I was three years old. Except for the time I was at school I have been in the saddle most of the rest of my life."

47

Miss Carlson's eyes were lit with a sudden interest. She had made a guess and she wondered if it could be right. "Where were you at school, Mr. Burns?"

"At a country school and four years in Denver," he told her.

So he was masquerading under a false name. She knew now who he was, Randy MacNeill. They had been in the fourth grade together at Edison School in North Denver. He was captain of the class baseball team. From the time she had first seen him this afternoon it had been nibbling at her memory that she knew him. Of course he would not remember her. She had been a fat nondescript little girl he had never taken a second look at.

The MacNeills were good people, respected ranch holders in Routt County. She wondered why he had dropped his name and taken another one. Probably he had got into some trouble and was a fugitive.

She had no thought of betraying his secret. Not yet at least, though it might be necessary to tell her uncle later.

Mrs. Edgar rose and glanced at the girls. "I think Robert has some business to talk over with Mr. Burns. Perhaps we had better leave them now."

She shook hands with their guest, told him she hoped he would come again soon, and herded her daughter and niece from the room.

Doctor Edgar wasted no time in getting to the subject in hand. "I understand from Sallie that you are trying to find where this young man MacNeill is hidden; that is, if he is still alive."

"That is right, sir."

"I don't know whether what I am going to tell you will help or not. On the day this MacNeill disappeared — that was Tuesday, wasn't it?"

"Yes sir."

"Well, on Tuesday I was called up into what we call the Hardscrabble country to take care of an old nester who had broken a leg. While I was returning, in late afternoon, I saw from a ridge four horsemen in the valley below. They passed into the timber beyond. On a ledge near the summit is a deserted cabin built by an old French prospector. The riders may have been making for that cabin. It would be a logical place to take MacNeill if they were planning to hold him prisoner because the country is practically deserted."

"Could you tell who they were?"

"No. I wasn't near enough. It was raining, too. But if these were the ruffians who kidnapped your friend I warn you that going near the place would be very dangerous."

"Tom has other friends beside me. We can

49

look after ourselves. You said it is a deserted country. You wouldn't expect to find four riders up there together, would you?"

"No. Unless it was a party of hunters."

"Could you draw me a map of the district with directions so that we could find the cabin?"

"Yes, I believe so."

Doctor Edgar found paper and a pencil. Randy looked at the map, asked a question or two, and was satisfied that he could find the prospector's cabin.

Before he left, the doctor warned him again to be careful. "From what my wife says I gather you think Metzger is involved in this business."

"It was just a guess," Randy said. "Your wife saw him go by with two other men. If they had captured Tom that would make the four you saw."

"If your guess is correct, you may depend on it that Metzger is acting for Johnston. I do not know what it is all about, but that whited sepulchre would not go as far as kidnaping unless he was prepared to murder if he thought it necessary. If you get the best of Metzger there is still Black Dillon, and Calhoun Ives who has the fastest gun in the country."

Randy nodded, knowing that what Doctor Edgar said was true.

Chapter Seven

There were three men in the Rubideau cabin. Two of them, Nick and Hank Sowder, were eating dinner at the table. The third, Tom MacNeill, lay on a bunk trying to read a tattered French novel the original owner had left when he departed. His ankles were tied together and a rope fastened them to a leg of the bed.

The fragrance of beefsteaks and coffee reached his nostrils and tortured him. He had not tasted food for four days. Apparently, he took no interest in dinner.

"How do you translate *mal entendu?*" he asked. "I learned only enough French in school to aggravate me."

Sowder glared angrily at him. He could neither read nor write and knew the prisoner was aware of it. "Keep your trap shut," he ordered.

Tom MacNeill turned a page. "An interesting story," he said. "You might enjoy it, Hank. A character in it reminds me of you.

51

He was guillotined — had his head cut off for his crimes."

Hank knocked over the stool he was sitting on as he rose to get at MacNeill, but his companion barred his way.

"Keep your shirt on, Hank," he urged. "He's just devilin' us. The guy has a right to be sore."

"He had better keep a civil tongue in his head," Hank snarled. "I don't have to take anything off him."

"Much obliged, Nick," Tom said. "It's a pleasure to have you for a jailer. When I get out of this I'll ask Sheriff Sanger to give you a job. Colonel Johnston may join me in recommending you."

"Fellow, you ain't never going to get outa this," Hank exulted. "End of the trail for you." He sat down and began shoveling in food.

"Why do you have to be so doggoned stubborn?" Nick asked the captive. "Looks like you must have worked up an appetite by this time. This grub sure goes to the right spot. Say the word, Tom, and I'll load up a plate for you. All you've got to do first is to sign that paper."

"I can't seem to crave food," MacNeill answered. "A doc once told me we'd all live longer if we ate less. I'm sort of trying out his advice."

"You ain't going to live long either way," Hank cut in brutally.

That was probably true, Tom reflected. Of one thing he felt sure. If he put his name to the paper selling his share of the Argonaut to Johnston he would be signing his death warrant. The banker would not risk letting him live. Of course the story given out later would be that he had sold his interest while he was in the bank. The deed was dated on that day, the previous Tuesday. Johnston would insist that Tom was afraid to face his partners, so he had taken his money and left the country.

Nick chided his fellow jailer. "No sense in you acting so mean, Hank. The boss told us all he wanted was for Tom to turn over his claim to this mine that belongs to the boss anyhow. He didn't aim to hurt Tom at all. All he asks is for him to be reasonable."

"Nothing could be fairer," MacNeill agreed. "A fine upstanding citizen, the colonel."

"Naturally you don't like him," Nick said. "I reckon you could call him a mite bossy when he's crossed. He aims to have his own way, all right."

From the first Nick had been unhappy about this business of starving their prisoner. He was sorry he had got into it. Maybe Hank was right, that the intention was to get rid of MacNeill finally. He had come to like the indomitable man on the bed. The prisoner showed no fear but on the other hand seemed to find pleasure in needling the thick-witted scoundrel Hank Sowder. More than once the big guard had been furious enough to throttle him.

The trouble was that Colonel Johnston had Nick roped and tied. There was nothing he could do to help MacNeill except slip him a drink of water at night when Hank was dozing. Nick was Johnston's man, had been ever since the colonel had gathered the evidence that would send him to the penitentiary or the gallows for robbing that bank in Texas during which one of his companions had killed the teller.

"I wish we didn't have to do this to you," Nick said. "It don't seem to me hardly human to starve a guy. If I had the say-so I'd turn you loose certain."

"Maybe you would like to tell the boss how to handle this," jeered Sowder, glaring at the bowlegged puncher. "Or I could tell him for you. He would like to know how you feel."

Nick rubbed his weak unshaven chin uncertainly. All his life he had followed the lead of stronger men. "I guess I talked out of turn," he admitted.

"A man has to play it the way the cards fall, Nick," MacNeill told him. "Take Mr. Sowder, for instance. When he first went visiting at the pen in Yuma he probably didn't like the change in grub. But after a few days — "

Sowder ripped out a savage oath and leaped to his feet, revolver in hand. "I don't have to take this from any man, let alone him."

Nick jumped for the man's wrist and forced the barrel of the weapon down. "Don't do it, Hank. Remember what the boss told us."

"That's right," Tom added. "His business with me isn't finished yet. But it was sure indiscreet of me to remind my host of the time he was guest of the government for two years just because he made a mistake and put the wrong brand on a few calves."

Rage stormed up in Sowder. He snatched the book from MacNeill and smashed a heavy fist into his face. Tom partially warded the blow with his left forearm and hit back with his right. Before Nick could stop his fellow guard the bully had hammered several pile-driving smashes at his victim. The eyes in Tom's bruised and bleeding face met those of the infuriated man scornfully.

"I'll live to see you hanging from a gallows," he promised.

Sowder broke loose from Nick and flung the book into the fire. "Damn him, I'll learn the fool," he shouted. "He talks big but before tomorrow night he'll be lying in the nearest arroyo with rocks and dirt tamped down on him."

"Remember what Metzger said," Tom reminded him. "Keep the deed handy."

"The boss ain't going to like this, Hank," the bowlegged puncher said sharply. "We got no orders to beat up this guy." He brought water in a pan and washed the bleeding face of the prisoner.

Tom said with a thin grin, "You're sure a softhearted killer, Nick. I'll have to get the hangman to do his job on you gently."

"You got me wrong," Nick corrected. "I'm no killer." He added reproachfully, "Why don't you act sensible and sign up? Then we could let you go as soon as Metzger shows up."

"Do you believe that, Nick, or just hope it's true?" MacNeill asked. "Where I would go is to that grave in the arroyo Sowder threatened me with."

"Soon," Sowder agreed ferociously. "I'll tell you something you don't know. Dolph Metzger will be along pretty soon, and his patience is getting wore mighty damned thin."

Chapter Eight

Randy MacNeill, Red Campbell, and Scanlan had been in the saddle a good many hours before they reached a ridge that led to the summit above the Rubideau cabin. Dusk had fallen and darkness was settling down over the range.

"I hope we have hit the right spot," Scanlan said. "All these hills look alike to me."

Randy did not answer. He was keyed up by an excitement which might easily turn to despair. There was no certainty that his brother was a prisoner in the old prospector's cabin. They might be hunting a mare's nest. He was less hopeful than he had been. Tom had probably been killed.

They worked carefully along the ridge, taking all the cover in the scrub oaks they could. If anybody should see them their chance of success would be lessened. At the edge of the timber which straggled up the slope they tied their mounts. Very cautiously they moved down the hill. Randy pulled up abruptly.

57

Smoke rose in a thin haze from the chimney of a cabin which stood out in the gathering darkness. As if somebody had given a cue, a lamp was lit in the shack.

"Stay here," Randy said. "I'll go down first and look things over."

"Why you?" asked Red. "If it's the way we think, hell may break loose in Georgia. Likely they have someone on the lookout. This is going to take all three of us or I miss my guess."

"It's my job. Tom is my brother. I'll sneak down right carefully and be back soon."

Young MacNeill trod down toward the house silently as an Indian. He slipped from tree to tree taking advantage of all the cover there was. When he was not more than forty yards from the cabin a man appeared in the doorway. Instantly Randy dropped to the ground. His heart beat like that of a frightened bird trapped in a man's hand. He must have been seen. The fellow was looking directly toward him. Then he realized that he was mistaken. The man was stretching his arms in a deep long yawn. He said something over his shoulder to somebody in the cabin, rolled and lit a cigarette, and went back inside.

Randy circled the house and reached it from the rear. He crept along the wall to an opening through which he could see inside. It had once been a window but all the glass was gone. Before he raised his head to look he heard his brother's voice. Tom was evidently taunting one of his captors.

"Even if they don't hang you, Sowder, you'll be sent back to the pen. That won't be so bad. Some of your old pals will still be there."

"Don't start that again, Tom," a voice implored. "Hank is already mad enough to bite nails."

A deep voice ripped out curses. Its owner was sitting at the table eating. He turned, swung an arm, and sent the knife flying across the room. The blade missed Tom and stood quivering in the log wall back of him. The ruffian flung himself across the room at the prisoner.

Randy's voice rang out sharply. "Hold it." He fired at the ceiling.

Sowder stared at the face in the window frame, hardly believing his eyes. His hand slid to the butt of his revolver.

"Who the hell are you?" he demanded.

"Put 'em up!" Randy ordered.

For an instant Sowder hesitated. Then he made his choice. His .44 flashed out and its slug ripped through the window casing. Randy's bullet tore into his belly and another

59

struck his throat. The fellow swayed, his feet clinging to the floor. His finger pulled the trigger again before he crashed down heavily.

Nick had made no motion toward his weapon. He stood, mouth open, chin fallen, muscles momentarily paralyzed by the shock of what had occurred.

"Drop your belt." Randy whipped the command out harshly. "Don't touch your pistol."

Nick's trembling fingers fumbled with the buckle and the belt fell. Young MacNeill put a hand on the sill and vaulted into the room.

"Back off to the wall," he directed.

Nick stammered, "Don't shoot," as he obeyed.

"Randy," Tom cried, astonished almost beyond belief. He had thought his brother was in Colorado on the Rafter K Bar roundup hundreds of miles from here.

Randy's gaze held fast to Nick. One glance had shown him that Sowder was dead. He stepped forward and kicked the belt under the bunk. "I need a rope," he said.

"Not for Nick," Tom told him. "He won't make us any trouble."

Randy took no chances. He made Nick untie Tom and with the rope bound the man's hands behind him. Before he had finished, Campbell and Scanlan burst into the cabin on the run with their revolvers drawn.

Red looked at Tom and cried, "The Lord be thankit. I didna think I would ever see you alive again, lad."

"Nor Randy either." Scanlan was still panting from the run. "I thought they had got him certain."

Randy walked to the bunk where Tom was sitting. He laid a hand on his brother's shoulder. He found no words to express the happiness swelling in him. For days his heart had been heavy with fear. The chance that he would find Tom alive had seemed to him slight.

"I had given up," Tom said. "I felt it would be the end soon, tonight if Metzger comes out here. And a miracle happened."

"I don't understand," Randy said, his voice shaken. "I was afraid — I didn't think — " He left the sentence unfinished. "Why did they leave you alive?"

"There is a deed on that shelf. I was to sign away my share of the Argonaut to Johnston. I knew that if I wrote my name there it would be my death warrant."

"Seven deevils are in the man," Campbell cried. "He thought that with you gone Ben and I would be feared to hold on to the mine."

Tom stood on his feet and caught at Randy to keep from falling. "Water," he croaked, his voice rough from a parched throat.

He drank from a tin cup and walked unsteadily to the table. "Except for a piece of corn bread Nick slipped me I haven't tasted food for four days," he said.

Coffee was still hot in the pot. There were biscuits on a plate and bacon in the frying pan. Tom restrained his voracious appetite. He knew his stomach was not yet in condition to take a heavy meal.

Campbell's stern eyes fixed on Nick. "This is an ill job you helped to do and we'll see you suffer for it."

"Don't be too hard on Nick," Tom told Red Campbell. "Nick was pushed into this. He didn't like it at all. When Sowder slept he gave me water. The food he couldn't get at, since Sowder used the sack of provisions as a pillow. He didn't trust Nick. When the fellow attacked me Nick fought him off."

"That may save him from prison," Campbell conceded, and quoted a verse of the Bible. "I was an hungered, and ye gave me meat; I was thirsty, and ye gave me drink."

"Is it likely Metzger will come here tonight?" Scanlan asked. "And does he come alone?"

"It is his night," Tom answered. "He comes late and alone. Doesn't leave Tail Holt till after dark so as not to be seen."

Randy looked down at the dead man on the floor and his heart sickened at what he had been forced to do. "We don't want any more killing," he said. "We had better get away from here if Tom can travel."

"There is no hurry," Tom said. "I'll eat again after a bit. I can make out to ride fine."

"Unless we want to wait and send Metzger to join his friend Sowder," put in Scanlan savagely.

"No," protested Campbell. "We'll have none of that. 'Vengeance is mine,' saith the Lord."

"I don't mind giving the Lord a helping hand," Scanlan said.

Within the hour they were in the saddle. Nick rode with them. In spite of Tom's assurance that Nick would give them no trouble, Scanlan rode directly behind the bandy-legged cowboy, his gun in his hand.

Chapter Nine

Dolph Metzger rode across the valley under a star-studded sky. He was bringing a definite order to make an end of this business. It was not safe to keep Tom MacNeill a prisoner any longer, nor was it safe to free him. He would give the man a last chance to sign over to Colonel Johnston his interest in the Argonaut, but it would make no difference to the stubborn fool whether he did or did not sign. The fellow had to be rubbed out.

As he came to the farther end of the ledge that held the Rubideau cabin he saw that there was no light showing in the windows. It might be that the kerosene in the lamp was running low. He shouted a hello but got no answer. Probably both guards were asleep. This annoyed him. It was contrary to the instructions given them, that one must be on the alert all the time.

He knocked on the door with the end of his quirt. No sound came from within. His angry call to Sowder to get up and light the lamp was unheeded. A vague alarm filtered into his mind. Yet there could not be anything wrong.

Metzger pushed open the door and stepped over the threshold. A man lay on the bed apparently asleep. But where were his guards? Had they killed the prisoner and left? Back of his anger was a growing fear.

He lit the lamp and what he saw gave him a dreadful shock. The man on the bunk was Sowder. The guard lay there dead with his mouth open. Nick and the prisoner were both gone.

Metzger blew out the light at once. Enemies might be lying in wait to kill him. He crouched in the darkness a long time, nerves tense, a crawling fear knotting his stomach with an icy grip. The barking of a coyote in the still night made him jump.

Through the window he could see that there were no horses in the corral. His own mount was grazing on the scant grass near the cabin. He made up his mind that whoever had killed Sowder had left.

But fear lingered in him, for he could not be sure that the killers were gone. Softly he opened the door a few inches and peered out, his searching eyes sweeping from right to left and back again. He bolted into the open, reached his horse and swung into the saddle, then jumped the animal to a gallop. Fear was still riding his heavy shoulders. Spurs roweled the flanks of his mount as he drove it through the brush. The cruel spikes of the prickly pear and cholla ripped his trousers and tore the flesh of his calves. Not until he was out of the valley did his panic subside.

The light of the coming day was driving back the darkness when he reached Tail Holt and knocked on the door of Colonel Johnston's house. His urgent hammering brought Black Dillon to an upstairs window.

"Where is the fire?" the gunman asked.

"Let me in. I've got bad news. Wake up the colonel."

Presently Dillon opened the door. "Did you have to wake us in the middle of the night?" he asked with cold sarcasm.

Johnston sat on his bed half dressed and listened to Metzger's story. This was a disturbing and alarming development, the first setback in his climb to local dictatorship.

"Who could have done this?" he asked.

"Somebody who followed Dolph to the cabin on one of his trips," Dillon jeered. This misadventure pleased him. There was jealousy among the top men in the Johnston regime.

"No," Metzger denied. "I checked plenty to make sure nobody was tailing me."

"The question is who, not how," Johnston reminded them sharply.

The most obvious suspects were MacNeill's partners. But how was it possible for them to have found out where their friend was hidden? And what had become of Nick? He might have double-crossed his employer, killed Sowder, and lit out with MacNeill.

"I never trusted him," Metzger said to Johnston. "But you picked him for the job. You would have him."

"It wasn't Nick," the colonel snapped. "He is probably lying dead in some arroyo."

Johnston spoke plaintively, but he was not himself convinced. He would not admit it to Metzger, but he might have made a mistake in thinking that the man was too weak to revolt, too fearful of being turned in to the Texas Rangers for the bank robbery in which he had been involved. Of course the fellow hated him, but he had discounted that on account of his timidity.

"You are overlooking the Halloran gang," Dillon contributed. "They have been our enemies for quite some years. This would be right up their alley. They are always ranging the hills and might easily have noticed smoke from the cabin. And for all you know these birds at the Argonaut may have thrown in with them."

Johnston did not like to think so. His feud with the Hallorans ran back to the Indian days. Dan Halloran was the first man to drive cattle into High Grass Valley. He had fought the Apaches in their intermittent raids. By the time Johnston had come into the lower part of the valley the Indians had been confined to reservations.

The colonel brought only a small herd but it grew with amazing rapidity. Halloran objected to his neighbor crowding the range with stock. He had served notice that this had to stop. The next day he was found dead in a gulch. He had been shot. His son Butch was a boy and no match for Johnston and his arrogant riders. The youngster's cattle were crowded into a strip between two prongs at the upper end of the valley.

Gradually a bunch of lawless men, cowboys and nesters who had been victims of the colonel's greed, gathered around young Halloran and preyed on their enemy's herds. They were a group who lived outside the law, particularly outside the law as Johnston interpreted and administered it.

The colonel sighed. He was wearing his most sanctimonious look. "I don't know why a man who spends himself building up the country can have so many enemies."

"Meaning what man?" inquired Black Dillon. He liked to needle his employer when the latter took on the role of piety.

Johnston ignored the question. "Envy and greed are evil qualities. When they go too far it is my duty to repress them."

"Sure," scoffed Dillon. "If you know who to start repressing right now. You can't take on at the same time all these bad characters that hate you."

"No matter who he got to help him this Tom MacNeill is responsible for the killing of Sowder. He must be punished."

"Not that you give a damn about Sowder," Dillon said. "Point is that this fellow is a game guy and will stand up for his rights. That's bad, ain't it, Colonel?"

"Are you on my side or his?" Johnston demanded angrily.

"I'm your paid rattlesnake stomper, Colonel," Dillon answered. "But my job don't include singing hymns with you."

"MacNeill probably has gone back to Three Cedars. He'll be on the alert and his two partners are tough characters."

"I like 'em tough," Dillon said. "Are you figuring that I'm to clean out all three?"

"Not necessary. With that scoundrel MacNeill out of the picture the others will throw in their hands. They will realize they can't blackmail me. I'll raise the price for their claim a little."

"Don't be too generous, Colonel," the gunman drawled. "This vein they have struck might peter out after you have collected a couple of hundred thousand bucks."

Johnston choked down his rage at this insolent gunman. He could not afford to quarrel with him now. The man would want a bonus for ridding him of MacNeill and he must bargain with him to keep the price as low as possible.

"I am sorry for this young man MacNeill," the colonel said. "But we can't have him murdering our friends."

In Dillon's cold eyes a gleam of sinister mirth showed. "Your friend, not mine," he corrected. "If you want my opinion Sowder was a mix of coyote, skunk, and wolf. Good riddance, I say."

"If we don't act fast they may get some of the rest of us," Metzger said.

"That is true," the colonel agreed.

They put their heads together to consider ways and means, after which Johnston spent fifteen minutes trying to make Dillon see that this would be an easy mission, the charge for which should be low.

"If you don't like my terms," Dillon said, "send Calhoun Ives. You don't want me more than ten feet away from you anyhow."

"I can't spare Ives from the Wagon Wheel," Metzger objected.

70

"No, you are the man," Johnston said to Dillon. "I tell you there is no danger for you, so why should I be held up?"

"I will tell you why," Dillon said. "We don't know how much backing this fellow MacNeill has. Plenty would be my guess. I can't go picking a row with him and then pump lead into him, not when his friends can prove you kidnaped and starved him. I would be in a hell of a jam. It must look like someone unknown had done it." The killer slanted half-shuttered mocking eyes at Johnston. "Of course I understand that if you got in a tight about it you would throw me to the wolves to clear yourself."

The colonel lifted his hands in a gesture repudiating any such thought. "My friend, you have a poor unjust opinion of me," he said reproachfully.

Dillon retorted, not without scorn, "I'm not worrying. I'll not throw down on myself. There won't be any evidence against me."

"No. We'll have an alibi watertight for you." Johnston shook his head sadly. "I don't like this. I'm a peaceable man. But what can I do when a man is robbing me but stop it?"

"You sure talk nice, Colonel," Dillon said with gentle irony. "Real nice."

Chapter Ten

The riders dropped down from the high country to the lower foothills by way of a canyon through which water tumbled in the rainy season. Randy looked at his brother solicitously. Tom sat the saddle with no sign of fatigue but though he had eaten twice before leaving the cabin he must be very tired. Four foodless days weaken a man.

"We'll camp in High Grass Valley," Randy said. "Nick says it is over the next ridge."

"That will be fine," Tom answered. "I'll sleep round the clock."

The sun was up hours before Tom awoke. They had brought food with them from the Rubideau cabin. The others had already eaten but Randy prepared a breakfast for his brother. Tom cleaned his tin plate twice before he had enough.

"What are we going to do with Nick?" Campbell asked.

The man had been kept bound during the night but with the coming of day he had been freed of the rope.

"We'll have to take him to White Rocks and turn him over to the sheriff," Scanlan said.

"For trial or to give evidence?" Tom inquired.

"For both," Scanlan answered.

Tom shook his head. "His evidence won't touch Johnston. Sowder is dead. That leaves only Metzger, who will swear he was never near the cabin and had nothing to do with the kidnaping. Johnston will cook him up a nice alibi. He wouldn't be convicted. Besides, I don't want to get Nick into trouble. I am convinced he saved my life."

"If we turn him loose he'll run to Johnston and tell him all he knows," Scanlan said.

"I don't think so, Ben. He knows that Johnston would likely turn his anger on him and have him badly beaten up."

Nick was sitting by the fire drawing pictures in the sand with the sharp point of a branch from a dead tree. He broke his silence with bitter words. "I'll never go near that devil again as long as I live. I took it on the lam here from Texas on account of some trouble I got into. He found out about it and has made me live in hell ever since for fear he'd tell."

"That is true. Sowder taunted him with it."

Tom spoke to Nick. "Where would you go if we turned you loose?"

"Would it be all right if I joined up with Halloran's bunch?" he asked timidly. "I can't go back to Texas."

"Do you know Halloran?"

"I've met him and two or three of his gang. They are not bad fellows if they do rustle some of the colonel's calves."

"How come he to be a colonel?" Randy asked. "Was he in the war? Johnston, I mean."

"I dunno." Nick scratched his head as an aid to thought. "Story I heard is that he hired a substitute to fight for him and when he moved here he figured it would be nice to be a colonel. So he kinda elected himself one."

"Why didn't he call himself a general?" Scanlan asked sourly. "I packed a rifle over my shoulder three years and came out a private."

"With a Confederate bullet in your leg," Tom said. "You didn't pick the right kind of parents, Ben. If your father had been a senator you might have come out a colonel like Johnston."

"He couldn't come out if he never went in, could he?" Scanlan growled. He was a short broad-shouldered man in his late forties, inclined to be irascible and a little difficult.

"Getting back to Nick," Randy cut in, "I

74

reckon it's not our business where he goes providing it's not Tail Holt. I'd advise him to hit the trail for New Mexico or Colorado. But that is his lookout, wouldn't you say?"

Scanlan differed. "It would be your lookout if he skedaddled back to Johnston and told him you killed Sowder."

"Nick isn't going to do that, Ben," Tom said. "But for his own safety Nick had better light out from this territory and get a job somewhere else."

Campbell's eyes picked up a rider topping the ridge in front of him. "A visitor coming to welcome us," he mentioned.

The stranger was a lanky fellow in shiny leather chaps. In spite of the big Mexican sombrero he wore, his face was darkly tanned by the desert sun and wind. The butt of a .44 projected from a pocket attached to the right leg of the chaps. He drew up by the campfire and shifted his weight to ease himself, part of it resting on the stirrup. He sat tall in the saddle, his hands cupping the horn. Though he showed no concern, his bleached blue eyes took in the campers vigilantly.

"Right smart increase in the population of High Grass Valley," he suggested. "Reckon there isn't a sheriff among you."

Tom guessed this long-legged rider was one of the Halloran bunch. "Nary a one," he drawled. "You lost any?"

"Not so you could notice it." The words dragged whimsically in response to Tom's friendliness. "Last time I saw one he was lookin' for me and I was movin' kinda fast away from him. Of course I was innocent, but hadn't time to explain that."

Randy laughed, replying with a misquoted tag from a school reader that had stuck in his mind. "Same here. We're all honorable men, Mr. Brutus."

"These gents are all right, Spud," Nick assured the cowboy.

"I would feel surer of that, Nick, if you weren't working for the Johnston outfit," the rider answered dryly.

"I done quit that gang, Spud."

"When?"

"Last night." Nick turned a puzzled face to Tom MacNeill. He did not know how much they wanted him to tell. He knew his reply had not convinced Spud that they were not Johnston's followers.

Tom saw no reason why they should not tell their uninvited guest the truth. His story omitted only two details, that his friends had found him through information obtained by his brother and that Randy was the one who killed Sowder.

Spud swung from the saddle much relieved. His intrepid bearing had been a bluff. He had been afraid this was a Johnston posse. Like most of the other residents in the district he had believed that Tom MacNeill had been killed at the instigation of Johnston. The escape of the victim and the death of Sowder pleased him immensely.

"Looks like we're all in the same boat," he said. "Come up and talk with Butch. He'll be plumb tickled at the way this came out."

Tom did not care to identify himself and his friends with reputed outlaws, so he declined the invitation tactfully. They would be glad to meet Halloran sometime but just now he was too worn out to ride an unnecessary mile. What he wanted was to get to bed and rest.

"Like to see you a minute," Nick said to Tom and drew him aside.

He wanted permission to leave the others and go with Spud. If he was seen with them later by any of Johnston's men the colonel would believe that he had killed Sowder and set Tom free. He could go with Spud and slip out of the valley across Cut Cliff Pass on his way to New Mexico. He would be safe and Tom's friends need not worry about his telling anything he knew.

Tom called to Scanlan to join them, knowing that Ben would be the one most likely to object to this. The man did not like the plan much. Under pressure from Butch Halloran the ex-guard might let out the information that Randy was Tom's brother and that he had done the killing. Nick promised earnestly that he would never tell anything about Randy to anybody. He was grateful to all of them for forgiving him and helping him to escape.

"Maybe I ain't much good," he said, "but I wouldn't rat on folks who have done me a kindness."

"That goes with me," Tom told him. "If it is all right with Spud you may leave with him. But don't stay with Halloran and his crowd. Keep traveling and make a new start."

There was no evil in Nick, Tom felt. He was the type of weakling whose manner of life took the color of his companions.

Spud looked Nick over with obvious distrust. "I don't know as the boys would thank me for bringing in one of Johnston's castoffs."

"You have it wrong," Randy said. "He has cast off Johnston."

Tom stressed again Nick's help in saving him. Spud gave in with a grin.

"I was one of Johnston's hired hands once myself," he admitted. "Several of our boys were. Let's go, Nick."

From the summit of the hill Nick waved them a goodbye.

Chapter Eleven

When the MacNeill brothers came to the summit of Soldiers' Pass the scattered houses of White Rocks far below reminded them of grazing sheep. From that height the main street was a narrow ribbon flanked on both sides by what might have been stones set along a garden path. The town nestled on the yonder slope of the cupped valley, every detail of it diminished by distance.

Tom glanced at the jagged outline of the range that was the far background of the panorama. The sun still rode well above the peaks.

"We'll make it in time to get a bath at Sim's barbershop before supper at Mother Gregory's," he said.

They had been in the saddle through the heat of the day and the men and their mounts were sweat-stained and weary. After the night camp in High Grass Valley they had separated from Tom's partners, Campbell and Scanlan to return to the mine at Three Cedars, the MacNeills to arrange shipment from White

79

Rocks to the Argonaut of a new cage with guides to replace the battered lift they had built themselves of odds and ends of timber. It had been ordered from Denver and ought to be already at White Rocks.

Before they reached the lower end of the ledge road long shadows from the cliffs above had crept down over the town. They crossed the grassy park and left their horses at a livery stable. After registering for a room at Mrs. Gregory's Trail End Hotel they paid two bits each and bathed at the barbershop. Randy gave his name as Lloyd Burns.

Those sitting at the long supper table of the hotel were all men. Two or three were brown cowboys in from the range to blow in their hard-earned wages at the bars and gaming tables. Others were store clerks, merchants, or faro dealers. One was a hard-eyed thin-lipped fellow whose gaze rested several times on Tom.

Randy murmured to his brother as he passed him a plate of hot biscuits, "Slit-eyed gent wearing a bowler hat takes an interest in you."

"I've been noticing that," Tom answered. "Must have seen me before."

"Nice manners, wearing his hat at the table," Randy commented. "Mrs. Gregory must appreciate that."

They gathered later that she did. After supper Tom stopped to say a few words to the hotel owner. She was a middle-aged woman with graying hair whose kindness reached out to anybody in trouble. She had carried on the cuff a dozen cowboys who were penniless and nearly all of them in time paid her what they owed. This untiring care for those in need or ill had earned her the title of Mother Gregory.

Randy asked her the name of the man wearing the bowler hat.

"He calls himself Clift Walker," their hostess replied. "I don't like him, though I don't know anything against him except that he is a tinhorn gambler and has bad manners. I have told him he must find another place to eat when his week is up."

"Does he live in White Rocks?"

"He comes and goes. The man seems to have money, though I have never known him to work." She said, after a moment, "Are you interested in him?"

"No — except that he seemed to be watching Tom."

"Maybe because he has heard about your friend being missing. A good many people heard of that. It was even in our paper."

That gave Randy an idea. He mentioned it later to his brother. Colonel Johnston would almost certainly accuse Tom and his partners

81

of murdering Sowder. Why not get their side of the story into the paper first?

Tom thought that might be wise. He knew Eliot, the owner of the *Sentinel*, an honest man who had dared to attack Johnston's methods in an editorial. White Rocks was the county seat, a larger town than Tail Holt, and though the colonel was influential there he did not dominate it as he did Tail Holt.

Between Jim Eliot and Tom was a mutual liking. The editor had a homely wrinkled face that had at least integrity to recommend it. He dressed carelessly, almost shabbily, in a seersucker suit that looked as if he slept in it. He was an old-timer, past sixty, a good citizen, blunt and fearless. Even his enemies respected him.

"Heard you had been found," Eliot said. "Didn't think you were tenderfoot enough to get lost."

Tom told him the story of his kidnaping, his captivity, and his rescue. But he left Randy entirely out of his narrative. His account was not strictly true. It conveyed the idea that a party of hunters had found him and had been forced to kill Sowder.

"Did these hunters have any names?" Eliot asked skeptically.

"I forgot to ask them," Tom answered. "That was sure dumb of me."

Eliot grinned. "I'd better put it that these hunters were strangers from Tucson." He understood why MacNeill did not want to implicate his friends. Johnston was not likely to take this lying down.

Tom started to leave but turned to put a question. "Know a fellow named Clift Walker?"

"Yes. He's a no-account scamp who ought to be run out of town. They claim he supplies whiskey to the Apaches on the reservation." Eliot asked with bland innocence, "Was he one of the hunters from Tucson?"

"No. Never met him until last night. He was eating supper at Mother Gregory's. He didn't say a word to me, but his eyes certainly drifted my way plenty. My guess is that he was surprised to see me."

"Figured you ought to be buried in a dry gulch with rocks piled over the grave?"

"Something like that. A little shocked that he had been given the wrong tip."

Eliot said with cheerful malice, "I would have given six bits to have seen good Colonel Johnston when he learned your demise was postponed."

"I don't like that word postponed," Tom said. "You make it sound like the day after tomorrow."

"Son, maybe I'm all wrong, but my advice

is for you to go heeled and keep your eyes skinned all the time. Johnston wants the Argonaut and you are in his way."

The editor watched with misgivings the young man leave. This was not the time for MacNeill to be intrepid and carefree.

The mining supplies had not yet arrived at the stage station though the manager had word that they had been shipped from Denver. It might be a couple of days before they reached White Rocks. The MacNeills decided to wait in town rather than go up to the mine and come back again.

Though they did not expect trouble, they never left their room without being armed. In deference to public opinion, which was opposed to the open display of weapons on the streets, they carried their .45's in shoulder holsters under their left arms.

During the daytime Tom and Randy took pains not to be seen together. It was possible that the owners of the Argonaut might need a friend unknown to the Johnston faction. For their meals they arrived at different times and did not sit next to each other.

Randy found himself sitting next to Clift Walker at supper the third day. It was the man's last meal there and he made occasion to be rude to Mrs. Gregory. Randy rose from his seat to protest but the landlady shushed him down. She did not intend to have any quarrel started about her.

"Want to make something of it?" Walker jeered.

"You will behave yourself in my house, sir," Mrs. Gregory said tartly.

A cattleman at the other end of the table spoke promptly. "Bet your boots he will. We'll see to that."

Walker knocked over his chair as he got up and went out of the room. He was sullen and angry but he did not dare to stand up to these men who were friendly to Mrs. Gregory.

Randy righted the upturned chair. "Pleasant gent," he commented. "Bites nails for his breakfast."

"Thank goodness, his week ends tonight," the landlady said. "He is the first unpleasant guest I have had. I hope he is the last."

Chapter Twelve

Clift Walker went his heavy-footed way down the street and turned in at the Good Cheer Saloon. Sitting alone at a table near the rear he saw without surprise a man whom he knew

85

slightly by sight. The man was Black Dillon.

"I'm Clift Walker," he said.

"Sit down." The words came curtly from thin lips that scarcely moved. Cold blue eyes drilled into those of Walker. They were taking nothing for granted.

The tinhorn felt a chill of apprehension, though this notorious killer could have nothing against him. He thought he knew what business had brought Dillon here. But there was a quality of still deadliness in the man from Tail Holt that disturbed him. He took a chair opposite the other.

"You sent word to Colonel Johnston that this Tom MacNeill is here. Is that true?" Dillon demanded.

"Yes, sir. He's here all right. Half an hour ago I was eating supper at the same table with him."

"Why did you write to Johnston?"

"I've had some dealings with the colonel. I figured he might like to know."

Walker pulled a newspaper from his pocket and showed Dillon a story in it. "The *Sentinel* got on the street this afternoon. It comes mighty near saying that Colonel Johnston was fixing to have MacNeill killed when some guys rescued him. Doesn't give his name but hints mighty loud."

"When did MacNeill reach here?"

"Came in Monday night, I think it was. Alone, far as I know. Neither of his partners were with him. Seems he is here expecting some mining machinery."

Dillon flung curt stabbing questions at Walker. Where was MacNeill putting up in town? During the day where did he hang out? Was he ever seen on the street after dark? If so, was he alone? Had Walker heard the names of any of the men who had rescued him?

The tinhorn gambler answered as best he could. The only accurate information he could give was that MacNeill was stopping at the Trail End Hotel. The gunman ordered him to watch the man and report his movements to Dillon.

"And if you want to keep on living padlock your tongue," Dillon warned, his voice soft and deadly. "I'll take care of MacNeill, and you don't know anything about it. You haven't even seen me in town."

"You can depend on me, Mr. Dillon," promised Walker, his voice humble and ingratiating. "Soon as this fellow MacNeill walked in for supper at the hotel I reckoned maybe I had better let Colonel Johnston know. The way I figure it this guy is a troublemaker and needs cutting down to size. I'll keep an eye on him for you and report."

Dillon was a stranger in the town. Nobody

who lived there was likely to recognize him. But he wanted to finish as quickly as possible what he had come to do and then leave immediately.

"Get busy right away," he told his spy. "Soon as you have got him spotted let me know. I'll be waiting here."

Walker lingered. He wanted some mention of pay. "What do I get out of it, Mr. Dillon?"

"You will be sent twenty-five dollars by mail."

"Who will send it?"

"None of your business. Get out and start earning it." Dillon's low lethal words were a spur to action. The man was dangerous when crossed.

When Tom MacNeill came out of the Trail End a man was lurking in the deep alcove entrance to a store on the opposite side of the street. The man followed him at a distance. Randy MacNeill stepped out of the hotel and recognized Clift Walker. Tom stopped to look at a pair of chaps hanging in the window of a saddler's shop. The gambler also halted and did not start again until Tom began to move.

Randy did not understand this and he did not like it. The fellow seemed to be dogging Tom. Was he by any chance one of Johnston's men? Young MacNeill kept pace with Walker about twenty-five yards behind him. Randy's unease had not reached the point of fear. He did not think this tinhorn had the nerve to go into a shooting affair even from ambush.

Darkness was beginning to fall before Tom reached the station. The manager was just closing the office but he told Tom that the mining shipment had arrived an hour earlier on the stage. He could get delivery next morning.

After Tom left the station Randy stepped out from the shadows of a cottonwood grove and intercepted him.

"That fellow Clift Walker followed you from the hotel clear across town. He dropped into a saloon couple of hundred yards back. I wonder what his game is."

Tom did not give much weight to this. Walker was a bummer of no importance. If assayed he would turn out all waste rock.

"I reckon so," Randy agreed. "But keep a sharp lookout. I'll be right behind you."

The lanterns in front of the saloons had been lighted and there could be heard and seen evidence that the night life was beginning. More men were on the street and as they passed the gaming houses the sawing of fiddle and the clicking of poker chips sounded.

A barefoot boy on his way home was singing the song that just then was having a great vogue in the Southwest:

> *"Jesse had a wife,*
> *A lady all her life,*
> *And the children they were brave —* *"*

Tom slapped the lad lightly on the buttocks and picked up the song with him.

> *"But the dirty little coward*
> *Who shot Johnny Howard,*
> *They have laid Jesse James in the grave."*

A man carrying a rifle had come out of an alley. He fired while the words were still on Tom's lips. Tom staggered and pressed one hand against the wall to keep from falling while with the other he groped for the butt of the .45 hanging in his shoulder holster. He got the weapon out and fired as he was slowly sliding down. The crack of the rifle boomed again. Tom's body plunged to the sidewalk.

Randy had not been far behind him and he came forward fast, firing as he ran to deflect the attention of the assassin. The ambusher had taken some steps toward his victim to make certain of the kill but he pulled up abruptly and swung his weapon for a shot at Randy who was still a moving blot in the darkness.

90

The killer became aware of men crowding the doorways both behind and in front of him. He could not wait any longer without being recognized and since his job was done there was no need to stay. His saddled horse was tied in front of the Good Cheer. He pulled the slip knot and swung to the saddle, jumping his mount to a gallop. A bullet tore into his arm but did not stop him. He went down the street and disappeared. In his hurry the hat was knocked from his head. Jim Eliot stepped out of the *Sentinel* office and picked the hat up from the dusty street where it lay.

Randy knelt beside the lax body of his brother. There was no stir of life in it. A voice sounded behind him.

"Move aside, young man. I'm a doctor."

Young MacNeill did so. He said, in a low stricken voice, "He's dead."

The doctor slipped a hand under Tom's vest and felt a faint beating of the heart. "Not yet," he differed.

"Save him, Doc," Randy implored. "He's my brother."

What could be done where Tom lay the doctor did, then had him carried very carefully to the Trail End Hotel. At midnight the wounded man was still clinging to a frail thread of life.

Chapter Thirteen

Doctor Edgar finished changing the dressing on the wounded arm of Black Dillon. He did not believe the gunman's explanation that he had been hunting and accidentally shot himself. Dillon was right-handed and the wound was just below the right shoulder. Also, the bullet had entered from the rear. Even a contortionist could not have fired the weapon. But he did not argue the point with his patient. Since the man was not a fool he did not expect the doctor to credit the story. All his arrogance demanded was that Edgar pretend to accept it.

The physician would have preferred not to have Dillon as a patient but he was the only doctor in town. The man had aroused him in the middle of the night. He had evidently come many miles on a spent and weary horse. It was apparent that he had been shot five or six hours earlier. Robert Edgar wondered where he had been and who had fired the bullet lodged in his arm. Part of that question

Dillon could not have answered. He did not know nor would he recognize if he saw him again the stranger who from the shadowed darkness had attacked him.

There was no cordiality between patient and doctor. They had exchanged only the most necessary talk concerning the treatment of the wound. On later visits both men continued their stiffness.

When Doctor Edgar finished changing the bandages for the last time, Dillon drew from his pocket two gold coins and flung them on the desk.

"Your fee," he said sullenly. He was in a bad mood and had been from the hour when he had been driven out of White Rocks. It hurt his pride to have fled wounded from the place.

The doctor pushed the gold back across the desk to Dillon. "My fee is six dollars," he said stiffly.

"Keep the change."

"No thank you. I will accept only the usual price."

Dillon glared at him angrily. "What if I won't have it that way?"

Edgar's eyes met his steadily. "I set my price, sir." He added quietly, "If you have any more trouble with the arm be sure to let me have a look at it."

Colonel Johnston's guard did not like this casual treatment. It diminished his importance. His was a special case and he wanted to stress that by overpaying. Six dollars for three visits might be enough for a run-of-the-mill cowboy but not for a man whose name was a household word through the Southwest.

"It will be like I say," he insisted and strode out of the office.

Doctor Edgar took from his purse fourteen dollars in greenbacks, put them in an envelope, and paid a small Mexican boy a dime to deliver the envelope to Dillon.

As the doctor turned to go back into his office he noticed a horseman galloping toward town along the gunbarrel road. He was filling quinine capsules when Randy MacNeill burst into the room.

"So you're back, Mr. Burns," Edgar said. "I'm very glad you found your friend alive."

"Doctor, that scoundrel Black Dillon came to White Rocks and shot him. He's still alive, or was when I left." The young man's voice broke. "He is my brother. My real name is Randy MacNeill. He is awfully badly hurt. Won't you come and save him? Doctor Goodson thinks you can help. He is young and doesn't know much about wounds."

After a moment's consideration the doctor said he would go.

"Doc Goodson says he needs a good nurse," Randy continued. "I don't know how to take care of him. Do you reckon I could get Miss Carlson to come? I would pay her anything she asks."

The doctor said he did not know, that Randy had better go to the house and ask her. Meanwhile he would get his horse hitched to the buggy and bring it home ready to start.

Randy had one more request to make. He was still calling himself Lloyd Burns. Under his own name he could not come back to Tail Holt. That might be necessary later. Would the doctor please remember to call him Burns?

Young MacNeill found the cousins in the garden cultivating the rosebushes. Polly dropped the trowel she was using and clapped her hands. At the sight of him her eyes had brightened.

"We're so glad you saved your friend if it was you and I'm sure it was," she cried in all of one unpunctuated breath.

Ingrid looked at her soiled hands, laughed, and offered one to him. "I'm told that cowboys do all their work on horseback and despise tillers of the soil," she said. "You call them hoe men, don't you?"

"My father had different ideas," Randy

95

told her. "He used to quote to us:

*When Adam delved and Eve span
Who was then the gentleman?"*

"Did he say anything about when Eve delved?" Ingrid asked.

Polly would have none of this foolery. "Tell us about how you rescued your friend and had to kill that bad man." She gasped, her eyes shocked at the charge she had made. "I don't mean you — I mean some of those with you."

"Now, Miss Polly," Randy said, smiling. "Do I look to you like any Wild Bill Hickok?" He turned to the older girl, his voice and manner sobered. "I'm in trouble, Miss Carlson. Big trouble. A ruffian followed us to White Rocks and shot my friend from ambush. He is terribly hurt. Doctor Edgar is going with me to help him if he can. We need a nurse badly. There isn't anybody there I can get. Good nursing might save his life. Will you go with your uncle?"

Ingrid said, "I'm not very experienced but of course I will go. When does my uncle start?"

"In a few minutes. He is bringing the buggy here." His worried eyes met those of the young nurse. "I'll never forget this," he promised.

He wanted to get back to his brother as soon as he could and he set out for White Rocks without waiting for the others. Passing the Wagon Wheel, he caught sight of Colonel Johnston and Black Dillon going into the gambling house with Calhoun Ives. The guard carried his coat loosely over his right shoulder, the sleeve swinging free. A white bandage showed. A surge of hatred swept through Randy. He wished he had shot Dillon through the heart. If Tom did not make it he would settle the account with this villain.

After an examination Doctor Edgar did not think Tom's chances good. He had lost a great deal of blood and one of the bullets had torn into his flesh not far below the heart. The only comfort he could give Randy was that healthy outdoor young men like Tom often made amazing recoveries. The Tail Holt doctor stayed two days with the patient, and at the end of a week returned. He was much encouraged. Tom was not only holding his own but beginning to gain. During those days of doubt Ingrid Carlson never left the wounded man except for her meals and to take a short walk every day. She slept on a cot in his bedroom.

"If he lives — and I think he will — you can thank Ingrid for saving his life," Doctor Edgar told Randy.

"I know," Randy agreed. "She is wonderful."

Her uncle slanted an understanding look at him. Randy was not referring only to her nursing skill, Edgar guessed. The young man was under the enchantment of love. He could not keep his eyes from betraying his feelings for this long-limbed young sylph, apparently so unconscious of his adoration but nonetheless completely aware of it.

The men who ate at the table with her were nearly all unmarried and in their twenties. From the time she had entered the dining room on the day of her arrival all the hotel boarders had been keenly aware of her. Her beauty took them by surprise and stopped all talk while she walked with light grace to the chair reserved for her.

They recovered quickly from their diffidence and when she took her walks in the late afternoons one or another of them just by chance happened to be going her way. She had in the first few days received proposals of marriage from two susceptible youths, both of which she declined with thanks.

Ingrid told her uncle about them, her eyes gay with mirth. "They don't wait to find out what I am like or till I really know them. I think they are afraid somebody else will get ahead of them." She gave a little giggle. "I'm going to have some more before the week ends. I can read the signs."

"You are irresistible," the doctor told her. "Don't you know why?"

"Of course I know. This is a man's town with hardly any unmarried girls in it, but even though that is the reason it is exciting not to know when I'll be stopped on the street by a young man offering his heart and hand."

"You enjoy leaving a trail of broken hearts behind you," Doctor Edgar charged, smiling at her.

"There isn't a broken heart among them," Ingrid corrected. "They are just being complimentary to the new girl. But they are such nice boys. Somebody ought to import a carload of pretty girls."

Tom had the inside track. He was not impervious to her charm. Her ways delighted him. When she was out of the room he missed her and time dragged. She was a good nurse and knew how to make him comfortable. The touch of her cool fingers soothed him. There was warmth almost of tenderness in her low sweet voice reserved only for the men she was nursing. As he improved enough to be out of danger her solicitude vanished, to give place to a gay companionship that made his illness not only tolerable but pleasant.

When Randy would come into the room

and find her reading to Tom or sitting by the bedside playing checkers with him he knew twinges of jealousy. He was very happy that his brother was recovering but he could not help thinking it was too bad he did not have the broken arm he had once threatened her with.

Randy was in the bedroom when she announced that Tom could now do without her and she was leaving next day. He did not take any chance that someone else would be her companion for the walk she always took. He was at her heels the moment she left the hotel.

She glanced at him, assuming surprise. "Dear me, if it isn't the man who likes to be alone," she exclaimed. "I wonder if he owns the sunset as well as the Tail Holt creek."

"I'm willing to share it with you," he conceded.

"You are generous, Mr. Bird. Or is it Burns?"

"The name is Lloyd Burns, Miss Carlson. If you can't remember my last name perhaps you had better call me Lloyd."

"I might call you by your real name, Randy MacNeill," she suggested.

"So Tom told you," he said.

"No. I knew it the first day we met. I was in your class at the Edison School in Denver. You wouldn't remember me, a fat little monster of no importance, but of course I couldn't forget the great captain of our baseball team."

He could hardly believe that she had been in his class. She was the sort of girl to dream about, with fine-textured skin smooth as satin and long-lashed violet eyes in a face not to be forgotten.

"It's amazing I didn't know you," he said.

"Maybe I have changed a little," she offered demurely.

"You look so young to be a nurse."

"I might answer that you are a little young to be — what you are."

They were climbing a hill spur at the end of the street. The sun had set in a blaze of color back of the sawtoothed range. Even in Arizona one did not often see such a display as this. For a long moment they watched it in silence before Randy prodded for the implication back of her remark.

"What am I, except a cowboy greatly indebted to you?"

"This Black Dillon came to my uncle to have his arm dressed. You wounded him to save Tom, I have been told. And your brother talked while he was delirious. Nobody heard what he said but me. You killed that man Sowder."

His eyes searched hers to find the meaning back of the words. "You think I am some sort of desperado?"

"No, I don't think that." She looked at him, a worried frown on her face. She liked this lean sun-tanned man who wore his hat tiptilted jauntily. Though he had been living in anxiety most of the time since their meeting on the bank of the creek, there had been occasions when she had visioned flashes of a gay and reckless charm in him.

He was probably wild and certainly could be violent, as he had proved. That he was in love with her she knew. But she had no intention of letting her liking for him go too far. Someday she would marry but the man she chose would not be one who lived in an atmosphere that fostered sudden death.

"But I think that both you and Tom are in great danger," she continued, pleading in her voice. "You and he know that. Why don't you give up and leave? You have had a dreadful warning."

"You have forgotten that we are living in America," he told her lightly. "And in the West, where men fought Indians, scalawags, fire and flood but did not run from danger."

"Yes, I know that, Randy. But those days are past or ought to be, and one thing I haven't forgotten is that this dreadful man Johnston and his hired killers aren't living in that free America we know." She added, very

102

seriously, "Tom won't be a well man for months. You can't be with him every moment. Suppose a killer tries again when he can't defend himself?"

"I am taking him to Tucson. Nobody will know he is there."

"And you? Will you stay with him?"

"Probably not. I don't quite know where I shall be," he said, his steady eyes looking straight at her. "I will be quite safe as long as I am Lloyd Burns."

"If your enemies don't find out that you are one of Tom's rescuers."

He did not ask for her secrecy. In her bright and sparkling face he read a fine and gallant honesty that made it unnecessary.

"I don't think they will. They would not expect me to be at Tail Holt."

She flashed a startled look at him. "You are not going back there, to a town run by a nest of your enemies?"

"Nobody will pay any attention to a puncher on the chuck line."

"But why? It doesn't make sense. Why go there and endanger your life?"

He had told her more than he had intended to say. "If I go it will be only on a scouting expedition." Changing the subject, he thanked her awkwardly for her great help in saving Tom.

In him was an urgent desire to let her know his personal feeling for her, but he was sure it would be useless and he did not care to join the group she had rejected.

Chapter Fourteen

Randy walked into the Silver Dollar and presently wandered over to the chuckaluck table. He played the two, four, and six. His luck was in. He shifted to the five, won two doubles, and cashed his chips.

"Me for the hay," he said, yawning, and sauntered out of the side door. Here a stairway led to the rooms above and a hall to the street.

He took the stairs to the third floor and opened the door of the first room on the right. Campbell and Scanlan were seated at a table playing stud. They pushed their cards into the center at once.

"Thought maybe you hadn't got our message," Scanlan said.

"Yeah I got it," Randy answered. "Had to shake a guy before I came up."

"When did you get back from Tucson?"

Campbell asked. "And how is Tom?"

"Give him time and he'll be all right, Doctor Edgar says, but he was hurt bad and he won't be strong for quite a while. He'll be out of circulation for two, three months. Maybe more. I got in this afternoon. Tom will get lonesome, but I am not going back to Tucson unless I have to. I don't want to lead one of the colonel's killers to Tom if I can help it."

"Tom will make out," Campbell said. "The Lord be praised he is alive. I didna think for a while he would live."

"Neither did I," Randy said. "I reckon you two came down to get the cage for the mine."

"Aye, we did," Campbell replied. "And what aboot you, lad? Are you going with us to the Argonaut?"

"Not yet, Red. I'm going to Tail Holt."

"And what for?" the Scot wanted to know.

Randy sat on the edge of the table, one leg dangling. "We had better face the facts, Red. Johnston's killers did not get Tom. The colonel isn't going to let it go at that, unless we throw in our hands. He still wants the Argonaut. We can count on that. He'll wait a couple of weeks and then strike again. He can't get at Tom, so it will be one of you two — or both as soon as he finds out Tom is alive."

"That may or may not be so," Scanlan said. "He may figure he has gone as far as he safely can. But what has that to do with you going back to Tail Holt?"

"The man who shot Tom is Black Dillon. I recognized him and he dropped his hat with the initials B.D. on the band. Doctor Edgar attended to his wound. He says Dillon is sore as a wounded bear with cubs. Since he doesn't know I'm on earth he will go after you. That's where I come in. Perhaps if I'm on the spot I can find out in advance what is planned."

Scanlan reached for the bottle on the table and poured a drink into a glass. He pushed the liquor toward Campbell who also helped himself. Randy shook his head. "Not just now," he said.

"Here's to hell on a shutter for Johnston and Dillon both," Scanlan snarled.

Campbell drank to that. "I think Randy's right. They are no' through with us. If I were a blackhearted villain the way they are I would try to get them first."

"Fine, Red," Scanlan said bitterly. "And how? That gunslinger Dillon guards his boss day and night. And there are Metzger and Calhoun Ives and others. You would be shot into a rag doll before you ever reached him."

"Yes," agreed Randy. "But I wouldn't. An unsuspected man can get a guy guarded by a regiment if he wants to take the chance."

"Are you telling us you mean to get these

killers?" Scanlan jeered.

The gray eyes on the younger man, cool and hard, met those of Scanlan steadily. "If Tom had died I would have got them sure. I may anyhow."

"Just walk into the Wagon Wheel and knock them off, I reckon."

"There is law in the land, Ben," Randy said.

"Sure. Johnston is it." Scanlan's eyes narrowed. "Maybe you have the right idea, Red. If the damned scoundrel means to get us like he tried to get Tom we ought to move first. We could slip into Tail Holt, lie low, and watch for a chance to get at him or Dillon."

"Johnston would get word as soon as you hit town," Randy objected.

"Not if we rode in after dark."

"Even if you pulled it off and lit out hell-for-leather somebody would spot you. A big reward would be offered and you would have to hole up in the hills the way outlaws do. You wouldn't like that. And what would happen to the Argonaut?"

"No use discussing it," Campbell said. "We are not assassins like them."

"What do we do?" Scanlan demanded irritably. "Sit around and wait for Johnston to fix up some accident for us to get killed?"

"I have a plan," Randy answered. "I am going back to Tail Holt. There I am not known except as a cowpuncher foolin' around and blowin' in his wages. If I get close enough to the gang I might find out what Johnston means to do and warn you."

Scanlan shook his head. "You're plumb loco, kid. They will find out who you are and you won't last longer than a snowball in hell. Just because you have been lucky so far doesn't mean you are a match for that crowd. Some of them sleep with their fingers on the triggers of their guns."

Red Campbell put big dusty down-at-the-heel boots on a chair. He wore stained levis and a scuffed leather vest over a cotton shirt from which many washings had taken the original color. He squinted pale blue eyes at MacNeill. He thought, *This kid will do to take along.* "How do you figure on getting close to the gang, kid?" he asked.

"I don't know, but I have a hunch the chance will come if I am around to take it. If I could sell myself to Johnston as a gunman I would be on the inside."

Ben Scanlan scowled at the slim boyish figure sitting there so poised and sure. Randy was not yet twenty-one. Scanlan could have given him fifteen years of age. The miner was irritated but also impressed. He could not quite take this as a kid spouting off. More than once he had caught a glimpse in this young fellow of a quality incongruous with his age, a driving force, leashed and controlled, that suggested explosive danger.

"Talk sense, kid," Scanlan snapped. "First off, you don't fill the bill for one of Johnston's warriors. You are no cold-blooded gunslapper ready to kill at a word from him. When he asks for your record, if you ever got that far with your fool notion, do you aim to tell him you killed one of his scoundrels, helped a second one join the Halloran gang, and wounded a third? That would earn you a job with him certain."

"Maybe it is a crazy idea," Randy conceded. "But look at it this way. If I am in Tail Holt watching these birds there would be a chance for me to pick up some sign of the play they are going to make. What's wrong with that?"

"The only thing wrong with it is that if they caught on to you Mr. Randy MacNeill would be a gone goose," Scanlan said.

"If we lived in Boston we could call the cops," Randy argued. "Out here we have to stand on our own feet. I don't figure on getting caught. Anyhow, I'm going. I've decided that."

Red did not like to let this boy undertake this job of spying. He would be in constant danger of discovery. But there was a hard competence in him Red had not often seen in one so young, a coordination of mind and muscle combined with a spirit so indomitable that nothing but death could quench it. So he judged.

But there was something else that bothered Campbell. He said, "You saved Tom's life twice. If we let you go to Tail Holt and if you get killed, how could we ever face Tom again?"

"I am not going to get killed," Randy said.

There was nothing for Campbell to do but make him promise to play it close to his belly and not be foolhardy. If he saw any sign of danger he was to light out of Tail Holt *muy pronto*, and if he needed help, Campbell and Scanlan would be at the mine.

Chapter Fifteen

Randy swung from the saddle at the Elephant Corral and sang out, "Hiya, Limpy. The bad penny's back."

Cal Cotting's wrinkled sun-tanned face lit up with a grin. "Where have you been hellin' around so long?" he wanted to know.

"Seeing the world. How have things been in Tail Holt?"

"Everybody wearin' mourning," Cotting replied with obvious sarcasm. "We lost one of our finest citizens, that upstanding gent Hank Sowder. Some ruffian cut him off in the prime of his usefulness."

"Some party unknown?" Randy inquired.

"That's right. And to make our cup of sorrow full another sterling character, Black Dillon, got to monkeyin' around with an unloaded gun and shot himself from behind but fortunately not before he had rubbed out that desperado MacNeill who got lost and found just in time for the aforesaid Black Dillon to riddle him."

"You mean this MacNeill is dead?"

"Deader'n a doornail," Cotting affirmed.

Randy did not correct Limpy's mistaken impression that Tom was dead. In fact, it was exactly the impression he had sought to create when he had persuaded Jim Eliot of the White Rocks *Sentinel* to run an item in the paper saying that Tom had suffered a relapse and died. He hid his satisfaction and shook his head dolefully. "Too bad I missed all the excitement," he said.

"Didn't any of this sinful shootin' happen in this quiet Christian town," Cotting explained dryly. "You aimin' to stay this time?"

"I might. With so much gunfighting going

111

on, a fellow would be safer in a place like this where everything is peaceful."

Cotting slanted a suspicious look at him. He wondered how much this Lloyd Burns had been involved in the recent shooting.

Randy walked up Trail Street and dropped into the office of Doctor Edgar. The doctor was startled at seeing him.

"What are you doing here?" he asked. "You know well as I do that this place is bad medicine for you."

"Still looking for a job," Randy told him. "Anyhow, I've been thinking it might not be such bad medicine after all, Doctor. If you and Miss Carlson would keep mum about Tom and me it would be safer for us. The talk is that Tom's dead. I would like to let it go at that for the present."

The doctor promised that there would be no correction of this by him or his niece.

When Randy entered the Wagon Wheel it was roaring with life though the night was still young. A dozen cow ponies were tied to the hitch rack in front, their owners at the bar or taking a fling at some game of chance. Most of the gamblers were intent on the play but a number of those present were eyeballers* shifting idly from one table to another.

*An eyeballer was one who looks on at games but does not play.

112

Randy fell into talk with a Cornishman who worked at Three Cedars in Colonel Johnston's Molly Green. The miner talked freely about the camp but answered with a curt "No!" when Randy inquired about the chance of locating a claim in the district.

"Better get a job at the Molly Green if you go there," he said.

"I don't want to be a mucker," Randy explained. "No future in that. I want to be on my own."

"No room for you there," the Cousin Jack told him sharply.

"Why?" Randy asked innocently. He wanted to find out how the actual miners felt about the situation.

The Cornishman looked this tenderfoot over with impatience but with a slight sense of responsibility. This youth was so guileless that he ought to be warned. "Just take my word for it, lad," he said finally.

On Randy's face was a puzzled frown. "Seems queer. I don't get it."

The miner went one step further, looked around to see if anyone was close enough to overhear him, then lowered his voice almost to a whisper. "Young fellow up there got the same idea. He got in somebody's way — and quit living. That's all I've got to say." He turned abruptly and walked away to watch the faro play.

While Randy sauntered around the hall ostensibly interested in the games or taking a drink of beer at the bar he was very much aware of Johnston and his gunmen. The colonel was sitting in a game of stud at the far end of the hall near the stand where the musicians played. Not more than six feet behind him was his shadow Dillon. He was talking with the violinist but his shifting eyes covered warily all those close to the colonel. The man's arm was no longer bandaged. To Randy there seemed an insufferable arrogance in this killer. A bitter anger boiled up in young MacNeill but no sign of it showed in his still body.

Metzger was no doubt number two of Johnston's warriors. Another top man was the slender deft croupier, Calhoun Ives, whose cold black eyes wandered at times from the roulette wheel and the chips he raked in to rest on anyone who might make trouble. From his reputation and appearance Randy guessed that Ives was the most dangerous man in the wolf pack that Colonel Johnston had gathered around him, an opinion he knew Black Dillon would not share.

The manager Metzger was playing the genial host to the customers, drifting from one game to another slapping backs and making friendly talk. He laughed frequently, white teeth showing in a hard weather-beaten face.

Above the clatter of the chips and the sawing of the fiddle rose the beat of hoofs, notice that horsemen were crossing the wooden bridge over the creek on their way to town. A group of men pushed through the batwing door from the street. There were five of them. The leader led the others to the bar. He was not tall but heavily built, with broad shoulders. His face was dark and leathery.

Close at the leader's heels was a giant, a head taller than his chief with body in proportion. He had protuberant eyes and a dish face red-veined from dissipation. This must be Tiny Shep Steelman, a notorious barroom brawler of enormous strength. Though Randy had never seen him he felt sure of that. The man in front of him, now hammering on the bar with the butt of his revolver as he demanded a quick drink, could be nobody but Butch Halloran. The long-legged fellow with bleached blue eyes sauntering in the rear Randy had met before. He was the cowboy called Spud.

While the bartender was busy setting out the glasses Steelman turned to face the room, a bleak challenge in his crouched pose. A gun nested low in the pocket fastened to his chaps.

Randy was still at the far end of the bar nursing his beer. The low voice of a player

115

reached him. "Butch Halloran and his gang are all set for trouble."

A sudden stillness came over the room. The slap of cards, the rattle of chips, and the music from the stand had ceased. Spud lifted a foot to the rail and the soft jingle of his spurs broke the silence. The cold touch of fear swept the hall, for if guns began to roar in the crowded room it would precipitate a massacre.

Randy softly laid the beer glass on the bar and his hand moved closer to the butt of his revolver. Swiftly he had sized up the situation. Metzger and Dillon were at the far end of the room. Between Ives and the bar were a dozen players. An explosion was near.

"Just paying you a little visit, boys," Butch jeered. "Don't say we're not welcome."

Ives spoke, his voice low and chill but clearly heard. "Put up that gun, Butch, unless you mean war," he ordered.

"Take your drink and get out, Halloran, you and your gang," Metzger snarled. "You are not wanted here."

"We are not wanted anywhere by your boss, Johnston," Halloran retorted. "His idea is for us to get off the earth. It ain't a notion we agree to."

"Now, Butch, you know better than that," Johnston said. "We are neighbors in High

Grass Valley. Any little difference between us we can talk over."

Randy was surprised at the mildness of Johnston's voice. In it he read a suggestion of urgent fear. It was the first time he had seen behind the mask of pompous dignity that Johnston usually wore.

"Sure," Halloran retorted bitterly. "All you did was to murder my father, rob me of my range, and build your herd by stealing my stock. To hell with talk." He added harshly, speaking to Dillon, "Stay where you're at, Black. Tonight isn't the time for the show-down."

Dillon had started to move toward the bar, but the sharp command of the colonel stopped him. "Do as he says, Black. I don't want trouble."

"He doesn't want trouble, boys," Halloran scoffed. "He'll find it in his lap some day, but he don't want it there no sooner than he can help."

Steelman's ungovernable temper slipped the leash. His hand swept up, a .45 in it. Before he could fire, a revolver crashed. The giant dropped his weapon and stared in shocked dismay at his torn and bleeding hand.

Randy stepped closer, smoke rising from the barrel of his gun. His voice rang out cold and clear. He was facing the startled men at

117

the bar. "I'll cut down the first man who touches his pistol."

The cowboys from High Grass Valley were taken by surprise. They had not come for a finish fight but to throw a bluff of warning. The issue hung in doubt while Halloran made up his mind.

From the far end of the room came Johnston's shaky voice. "No more shooting, boys. Let us be reasonable."

Dillon waited, a .45 in his hand pressed close to his side. Ives was shifting his position to get a clear space for a shot. Men at the tables were ducking underneath or scurrying for shelter. Johnston, the first to seek cover, had dived back of the piano.

Randy's curt order cut into the confusion. "Take it easy. Nobody else is going to get hurt." In his unruffled words was a cool assurance. "You heard Mr. Metzger. Down your drinks and hit the saddle."

Halloran glanced at Steelman. There was no longer any fight in the big fellow. He was nursing his hand, wincing at the pain.

"I got to see Doc Edgar," he yelped.

"Fine," Randy said. "Have him fix you up, then hit the trail for home."

"Yeah, but this thing ain't ended," Halloran growled. "One of these days it'll be our turn."

The cowboys at the bar, faced by an unexpected crisis, had not known how to meet it. They were fighting men but they had not come to start a battle. The place for that would be on the range. Randy's instant domination of the situation and Halloran's acceptance of it had turned the scale for peace.

The bleached eyes of the long-legged puncher Spud met those of Randy with reluctant approval. The white teeth in his brown face flashed a grin. "Fellow, you're sure Johnny-on-the-spot. If Butch doesn't want to call your hand I pass." He picked up one of the glasses on the bar.

"Is this on the house, Metzger?" he quipped.

"Call it on the house and light a shuck, Spud," Metzger retorted. "But don't come back."

"Maybe you'll return our call," Spud said lightly. "If you do we'll guarantee you a right warm welcome."

The cowboys emptied the glasses and followed Halloran to the door. Spud did not join the retreat. He stood with his back to the bar, elbows resting on it and one foot hooked over the rail. The young scamp wanted it understood that though Halloran had given way for the moment, Spud was not knuckling under. There was a jaunty you-be-damned challenge in his pose and in his cool eyes.

He nodded a goodbye to Randy, said, "I'll be seeing you, fellow," sauntered to the door, and flung up a derisive hand before he disappeared into the street.

Randy slid the revolver back into its holster and started to leave by the side door. The croupier Ives was there before him.

"Wait a minute, kid," he said. "I expect the boss will want to see you." His dark eyes rested with a surprised respect on this youngster who had stepped in from nowhere to play the lead in a drama that had just skirted tragedy.

He led Randy through the crowd of excited chattering patrons. A little man wearing spectacles slapped Randy on the back. "You sure spread the mustard, young fellow," he chirped. Another told him that he sure was one wampus hell-a-miler.

Colonel Johnston had not quite regained his suave composure. In taking cover back of the piano during that dreadful minute when it seemed likely that a dozen guns might start smoking he had lost face rather badly. He was very pale and his pulse at the temples was throbbing visibly.

"I am under obligation to you, young man, for averting what might have been serious trouble," he said. "The Halloran gang are a criminal bunch of outlaws who hate me. I'll talk with you tomorrow. Come to my office at the bank about eleven o'clock."

Randy said he would be there.

As he left he heard Dillon's angry contemptuous comment. "Nothing to him. He had bullheaded luck, that's all."

The answer of Calhoun Ives also reached him. "I think you are wrong, Black. I would say the kid made his own luck. He strikes me as the kind who will go on making it."

Chapter Sixteen

Colonel Johnston's strength lay in his money and the guns it could hire, but even men who are willing to hire out as gunslappers cannot be depended upon to follow a coward. Black Dillon was an exception. He was the highest paid man in the colonel's organization. He was also the only man in the organization who fully understood the colonel. He was an insolent scoundrel, but Johnston accepted his insolence because he needed Dillon, and Dillon stayed on the job because the pay was good.

It was different with Dolph Metzger and Calhoun Ives. Both were staring at Johnston. He wondered if they sensed the fear that was in him. Then he wondered if they had seen him disappear behind the piano. He cleared his throat. He had to play this out.

"We cannot let this kind of thing happen again," Johnston said. "We might have had ten men killed here tonight. You can say that the kid had fool luck if you want to, Black, but it was fortunate for us that he did."

"There is one way to put a stop to Halloran's visits," Dillon said. "Spud invited us to return their call. Maybe we had better accept the invitation."

Johnston nodded agreement. "Perhaps that is what we should do."

"I'll ride to High Grass Valley," Ives said. "Any day that you want to lead us."

The gambler walked away. Johnston thought, *He knows I will never lead them.*

"I think I'll go home," Johnston said, and turned to the side door.

Accompanied by Dillon, Johnston walked down Trail Street toward his house. He was very nervous, now that he was outside, and his eyes searched every alley they passed. The guard was contemptuously aware of his fear.

"Some of the Halloran outfit might still be in town," the colonel said. "They might be hanging around to get me."

"So they might," Black Dillon answered.

"And we have no piano with us behind which you can hide."

Dillon was the only one of Johnston's men bold enough to fling taunts at him. This was an example of his insolence that made the colonel furious.

"You'll go too far some day," Johnston told him angrily.

"Any time you are not satisfied just say so and I'll quit nursing you."

"I didn't say I wasn't satisfied," the colonel snapped. "But you don't have to be so crossgrained and impudent."

They could hear the murmur of the creek running parallel to the street. As they turned from the business block to take the road leading to the house where they lived, there floated to them on the light breeze from across the stream an eerie high-pitched sound of singing. The words came faint but clear:

"But the dirty little coward
Who shot Johnny Howard,
They have laid Jesse James in the grave."

The fear the Halloran gang had aroused in Johnston had not entirely subsided. He clutched at the arm of the guard, suddenly frightened again but in a different way this time, a worse way because this was supernatural. "God, it's his voice" — the last words Tom MacNeill ever spoke.

Black Dillon was not afraid of ghosts. The shadows of those he had murdered never rose to trouble him. "Buck up, you chicken," he said scornfully. "It's some kid singing."

"It came from the graveyard over there. I — I don't like it. I tell you I don't like it."

"Hell's bells! What's the difference. Mac-Neill wasn't buried over there. Some fool kid on his way home, I tell you."

Another faint snatch of the song came to them with a strangely weird effect:

"They have laid Jesse James in the grave."

Coming as it did in the darkness of the night so soon after the trouble with the Halloran bunch, Johnston was completely unnerved. He had to set his chattering teeth to keep from running.

"Let's get away from here," he urged.

"All right," Dillon said. "We'll be home in a minute and you can hide in your wardrobe."

But the guard was not so unconcerned as he pretended. There was just a chance this might be some trap laid for them. He was pretty sure the words had not come from the lips of any boy. He walked with his hand on his gun butt, listening for any sound that was not natural, eyes trying to pierce the darkness that lay around them. He wondered if the Hallorans could have heard that Tom MacNeill had been singing this song when he had shot him.

They reached the house safely. Dillon would not have admitted it, but he felt better when a lamp was lighted and the doors locked. Johnston rarely drank, but as soon as he could, he got out a bottle and poured two glasses half full of whisky.

Black Dillon picked up one of them. Before his lips touched the liquor he offered a mocking toast. "To Tom MacNeill's ghost. May it lie buried with him deep in the grave."

The colonel was not so hardened a villain as his shadow. He said, "I must protest at such coarse levity. MacNeill forced us to do what we did but it was a regrettable fact and certainly no occasion for jest."

"Forced us, did he?" Dillon leered at his employer. "You don't need to worry. You can always salve your conscience by doubling your subscription to the church," he drawled.

Chapter Seventeen

When Randy MacNeill walked into the bank he wore a low-crowned black hat, a clean white shirt, a soft-toned silk bandanna, and a suit of the type known to cowboys as store clothes. The change in his dress was no more noticeable than that in his manner. He was no longer a fiddle-footed range rider come to town for a lark. The eyes in his lean grim face were hard as topaz.

The very respectful gaze of the teller revealed that he had heard, as most of those in town had, of his demonstration at the Wagon Wheel on the previous day. That suited Randy. He had taken the center of the stage for a purpose.

"Colonel Johnston said for you to go right into his office," the teller told him. His solemn voice intimated that only the most important persons were allowed such prompt admission.

The banker looked up from the letter he was writing and laid aside his pen. "Sit down, young man."

Randy took the chair on the opposite side of the desk. Johnston leaned back and looked the youth over with a view to impress. MacNeill casually got the makings from his upper vest pocket, rolled a cigarette, and lit it. The banker frowned. He did not like this nonchalance in his presence. Not many men could come in here and adopt such an attitude of equality and that was exactly what this cowboy was doing.

Johnston coughed. "Your name is Burns, I am told," he said.

"Correct."

Where were you living before you came here?"

"In Colorado."

"Just where in Colorado?"

The level eyes of MacNeill looked directly into those of the banker. "Here and there," he answered.

Johnston understood what they meant. The man was telling him to drop that line of questioning. He must be on the dodge, a fugitive from justice. If so, he might be of use.

"What you did yesterday took nerve," the banker continued. "And a swift presence of mind. You were in great danger. Halloran's ruffians might have riddled you."

"I had the drop on them," Randy mentioned.

"You had amazing luck from start to finish, first in shattering the pistol hand of the fellow Steelman."

"No luck there," Randy differed. "I was within fifteen feet of him."

"One man can't cover five. Nobody but a brash boy without experience would try it." Johnston's voice showed impatience. This young cowboy was far too cocky.

"We learn something every day, don't we, Colonel?" Randy said flippantly. "It can't be done, but a brash kid did it."

"If I hadn't ordered no more shooting they would have killed you," Johnston said gravely. "Never in your life were you in more danger."

"I'm certainly obliged to you, Colonel," Randy's derisive grin mocked his words.

"You seem to be the kind that knows it all," the banker replied. "That is your misfortune. The point is that I owe you something. Innocent men might have been killed and that would have distressed me greatly."

From his desk Johnston picked up some greenbacks lying there. He counted out thirty dollars, then after a momentary hesitation added twenty more. He pushed them across the desk to the cowboy.

Randy did not touch them. "No thanks," he said.

"You think that is not enough." Johnston

128

was plainly annoyed.

"I think it is too much. I did not butt in for money."

Johnston's gaze held in doubt to the lean brown face opposite him. "What for, then?" he demanded. "You had no chips in the game."

Randy leaned a forearm on the table and leaned forward. "You're smart, Colonel. I'll tell you why. Just sheer bravado. I wanted to attract your attention. Your eyes didn't even notice me when I passed in front of you. To you I was a two-bit cowpuncher. If I stay in this town I mean to be more than that. I want to work for you."

"What kind of work?"

"Work that is both soft and hard. Put it that I am lazy, that I would like to do my work loafing around." Randy's chill hard eyes bored into those of the banker. There was a kind of deadliness in the words that then fell softly. "Work that takes only a split second to do but has to be lightning quick and sure."

Johnston's surprise held him silent for a moment. "You want to be one of my protection men?"

"Call it that. I am a gun for sale."

"How old are you?"

Randy answered with a question. "How old was Billy the Kid?"

"That young villain was a topnotch gunman. They say he was the best man with a forty-five in New Mexico."

"You haven't heard Shep Steelman complain I don't shoot straight enough," Randy said dryly.

The colonel neither accepted nor discarded the idea of employing this hard young devil. With the Halloran gang ready to declare war, coming right into town as they had last night, and with so many more enemies who hated him he could use another tough warrior.

"I don't hire men just for emergencies," he explained. "They earn their pay at work and they have to stay in my organization long enough to show me they can be trusted."

"I am prepared to stay with you long enough so you'll find out what I can do," Randy said. "What I meant was that I am not a pick-and-shovel man. I would be worth more to you in a responsible position."

Johnston frowned. "And what I meant was that a man has to prove his worth before he is given too much responsibility. I demand of the men close to me absolute loyalty and also efficiency. When I give an order they do not ask questions but obey it."

A door leading to an inner room opened and Black Dillon came through it. His shallow stony eyes focused on MacNeill. Randy met his gaze steadily. He knew that this man reciprocated his hatred. The reason he could guess. Dillon was a top man in his field, a killer feared by other gunmen as well as by ordinary citizens. But yesterday it had been Randy in the spotlight who had quelled the trouble before it exploded into a battle. Fifty had seen this kid take the play away from him and strut his stuff. That was one thing Black Dillon could not forgive.

It did not matter that Dillon had been in no position to interfere. Men would talk about this upstart Burns and what he had done. Some of them might ask sarcastically where the great Black Dillon had been. The fear that he might lose rankled in the killer's arrogant mind.

Randy suspected that there was an eyehole between the rooms but he was not sure whether the bodyguard had come in of his own accord or been summoned by Johnston.

"You don't know nothing about this swollen-up pup, Colonel," Dillon said irritably. "I have been listening to his guff. After all what has he done? Yesterday he makes a grandstand play that wasn't necessary. I was ready to take over the situation. Pay him off and let it go at that. Let him nick you for fifty bucks. Or put him to work mucking at the Molly Green."

"Sowder has gone. Maybe I could use this young man." Johnston was arguing aloud to end his own indecision. "I don't want to be caught shorthanded."

"You have good men paid to take care of trouble," Dillon interrupted. "Men you know you can trust. What could a kid like this do for you?"

"I daresay you are right," Johnston said. He turned to Randy. "If you would like a job at the mine I'll give you a letter to the superintendent."

Randy rose. "No thanks. I see I made a mistake. I thought you ran the show but I see it is Mr. Dillon. Well, no hard feelings. I'll run out and have a talk with Butch Halloran. I reckon he can find use for me."

"After what you did yesterday?" Johnston asked.

"I'll explain I was just giving evidence he needed me." Randy's smile was chill. "No trouble to fix up a deal with him. The way I hear it he has no hired gunslinger telling him how to run his business. Be seeing you one of these days."

Johnston did not like the prodding Randy was giving him, but he did not want any more enemies handy with a gun. He said, "Don't push on the reins. I'll find something for you to do. The pay will be fifty dollars a month."

"For the first two months," Randy amended. "After that it will be seventy-five and special pay for any stomping-out jobs there are."

"I don't like this, Colonel," Dillon broke in. "Let me run this bird out of town."

Johnston ignored the suggestion. "You rate the value of your services high, Burns. You are not indispensable, you know."

"You wouldn't want a dollar-a-day man for the kind of work you might ask me to do," Randy said. "He wouldn't be tall enough in the saddle."

"For a young squirt you've got a hell of an opinion of yourself," Dillon said angrily. "What record have you got, except that grandstand play yesterday? For a dollar Mex I would guarantee to cut you down to size."

"I'll make that a U.S.A. dollar." Randy pulled a silver dollar from his pocket and laid it on the desk. "To find out whether your guarantee is good," he drawled.

The colonel lifted a hand quickly to restrain Dillon. He took another swift look at this slim long-backed bronzed youth with the mocking light dancing in his eyes. He saw a man unafraid, master of himself. If his reckless feet had carried him on forbidden trails he had always been ready to pay the price. So the banker judged.

Johnston picked up the dollar and handed

it back to Randy. "One thing you must understand to start with — and you get it too, Dillon. I won't tolerate any quarreling among my men. The first one who starts it gets his time. None of you can grind your own corn in my mill. Your jobs won't conflict. Dillon is my personal guard. I'll fit you in somewhere, Burns. But get that chip off your shoulder, young fellow."

Randy's grin was warm and carefree. "It's off already. Just one happy family."

"In that case you two had better shake hands to show there is no ill feeling."

Neither man made a move to offer his hand. Dillon saved the younger man embarrassment by flinging out a harsh refusal.

"I'll be damned if I do," he said. "We don't have to sleep under the same tarp because we both draw our pay checks from you. I don't like this bird. He's a show-off and I tell you you're making a mistake, but it's your say-so. If he's got sense enough to stay out of my way I'll let him alone."

"Looks like everything is going to be nice," Randy assured his new boss, no hint in voice or manner that hatred of them both was churning in his veins.

"It had better be," Johnston replied sharply. "Any fighting either of you do will be for me." He turned to Randy. "I suppose you are broke like all the cowboys. Stop at the teller's window and he will give you thirty dollars to be charged against the first month's wages."

"I had a little luck at the wheel, Colonel, and have enough *dinero* to carry me until I have earned my pay," Randy said. "No need for me to draw in advance."

"All right," his employer told him. "It will be waiting there for you when you need it."

Randy nodded and walked out of the bank. He had refused an advance because he did not want to put himself under any obligation to this man. He was a spy in the camp of the enemy. Though he had schemed to arrange this, he hated the position in which it placed him. Nothing less urgent than the reason that had moved him could have induced him to work for Johnston. On one thing he was resolved, not to take any money from him. If he was here more than a month he would let his pay accumulate at the bank and not touch it.

He strolled down to the Elephant Corral for a talk with Cat Cotting. The old man limped out of a shack he used for an office. His high-pitched falsetto flung out a cheerful greeting.

"What's this I hear about you single-handed wipin' out the Butch Halloran outfit?" he gibed.

"You don't want to believe all you hear,

135

Limpy," Randy cautioned with a grin. "All I did was nick a guy who had me scared."

"Tell it to me," Cotting said. He liked this slim lithe man, young in years but with a gay impertinence that masked a steely strength.

They sat on their heels in the shadow of the adobe corral wall.

"You do the talking first, Limpy," MacNeill said. "I want to know all about this Halloran bunch that you can tell me."

Cotting talked. It had been in the days when the Apaches were still raiding that Dan Halloran had driven his herd into the High Grass Valley. For half a decade he had fought off their intermittent raids. After the Indians had been confined to reservations Johnston had come into the lower end of the valley with a small herd that grew with surprising rapidity.

"The calves rustled from Halloran's herd, I reckon," Randy guessed.

"Mr. Burns, you shock me," the old man reproved him with a gleam in his eyes that did not look shocked. "Never forget that Colonel Johnston is our leading citizen, the source from which all blessings flow. Likely all his cows had triplets."

"His bulls too, probably, but excuse me, Limpy," Randy said gravely. "I regret an unworthy suspicion."

"Old Dan was one tough hombre but straight as a gunbarrel road. He had been right neighborly when Johnston first drove his stuff into the valley but he got mighty tired of the fellow's grabby ways. The story is that his riders caught Johnston and one of his scalawags branding a Quarter Circle D H calf after killing the mother. Dan was rarin' mad. He felt sure this had happened a good many times and he came pretty near hanging the two rustlers. But the thieves begged so hard for their lives that he let them go with a warning that this was a last chance for them. The next day Dan was drygulched. Understand, I'm not sayin' who did it."

"I understand," Randy replied. "I have already forgotten you mentioned the subject."

"Well, that turned the tide. Butch was just a kid then and no match for the colonel and his bunch of warriors. He come pretty near being put out of business. But in this country a man who sets out to make himself king has to run over a lot of little folks. Some of the wild ones drifted up into the rough district of canyons and groves above High Grass Valley and threw in with young Halloran. You will hear people say they have gone bad. Maybe so they do rob stages. I wouldn't know. But their raids on the herds of Colonel Johnston sure annoy him considerable. Still Johnston waxed

137

fat, as the good book says, and became very rich in cattle, in silver, and in gold. That's the story, son, and if you blab it as coming from me, I'll be in a heck of a fix."

"Don't worry about that. I hate this rotten outfit more than you do."

"Not possible." Anger blazed in the faded eyes of the old cowboy. "If I was half the man I used to be I would pump lead into the greedy scoundrel. Someone will give it to him one of these days. He has ruined more men than you can count on all of your fingers." The fire died from the wrinkled face. His war days were past.

Randy was disturbed in mind. He wanted to tell his old friend something without letting him know what it was. "You are going to hear something about me that you won't like to believe," he said.

Cotting stared at him. "I don't get it. What will I hear?"

The young man could not take the risk of giving him more information. Cotting was not only garrulous but loyal. In defending Randy from criticism he might say too much.

"You'll get it in a day or two. I hope we can still be friends."

"What the devil are you talkin' about?" demanded Cotting. "Are you aimin' to rob the bank or something?"

"You'll think it worse than that," Randy answered.

There was a frown on Cotting's face as he watched MacNeill go. Something about this worried him. Surely the boy did not have in his mind a crazy idea of killing Johnston or Black Dillon. What reason would he have? But only a minute or so ago he had said he hated Johnston's outfit more than Cotting did. Why? The old cowboy shook his head. He didn't know. But he was sure of one thing. The young fellow was asking for trouble certain.

Chapter Eighteen

The following morning when Black Dillon walked into the bank with his boss he stopped at the teller's window to pick up his wages, after which he followed the colonel into his office. He found Johnston staring at a paper lying on the desk in front of him. The banker looked up, shock and fear written on his face.

He said shakily, "Read this, Dillon."

Blocked out by a pencil on half a sheet of

139

bank stationery were the words:

The dirty little coward
Who shot Johnny Howard,
They have laid Jesse James in the grave.

"How come that paper here?" Dillon asked.

"I don't know," Johnston answered nervously. "Call Udell in."

The teller could give them no information. After unlocking the bank an hour earlier he had gone downstairs for about five minutes to open the safe and bring the cash up. Except himself nobody had been in the building unless it was during that short time. Udell returned to his work in the outer room.

Dillon shrugged his broad shoulders. "Don't mean nothing, Colonel," he said. "Just some more funny business."

"It does mean something," Johnston answered, the paper shaking in his hand. "It's a threat. Somebody does not want me to forget that Tom MacNeill was humming that song when he was shot. Whoever wrote that didn't mean Jesse James but young MacNeill."

"Say you are right. What difference does it make? That is finished business."

"This paper is to tell us it isn't finished."

"The guy that wrote it does not know who killed Tom MacNeill and if he did know there is nothing he can do about it. He can't touch you — not while I'm here." A thin smile lit the man's wolfish face. "I'd like to see him try it."

"Scanlan or his partner must have done this. How did he get here without being seen?"

"You are jumping at conclusions," Dillon said maliciously. "You don't have to go so far to find an enemy. There are plenty of men right here in Tail Holt — excuse me, Colonel, I mean Johnstown — who are itching to bump you off. But they know they dare not try it with me behind you."

"I don't want to think that. This town would be nothing without me. I have done a lot for it. Surely nobody here can hate me so much. They don't have any reason to hate me enough to kill me." The words were almost an appeal for the gunman to reassure him. He felt, as he often did, the sense of tightness in his chest, of a leaden weight in his stomach, born of fear flooding him.

"You mean you've done a lot for Colonel Amos Johnston," Dillon corrected, not taking care to keep the scorn out of his voice. "That is why you need me. Too many people tromped down by you. Any night one of them might cut loose."

Johnston did not like to think of that. He

always covered up in his own mind any thought of evil doing, preferring the illusion he had done a great deal for the town. Dillon's words added to his discomfort, so he harked back to the immediate subject in hand. "I feel sure that Scanlan and Campbell are back of this. The question is, what do we do about it."

"Rub them out," Dillon advised.

"I can't do that, not just yet. It's too soon after the MacNeill trouble, and it is a thing I do not like to have done. Why not send this Burns boy to Three Cedars to check up on Scanlan and his partner?"

"He is so brave with a gun he could get rid of both of them for you," the guard sneered.

"A man can't solve all his troubles with a gun, Dillon. That should be the court of last resort, to be used only when a man becomes too unreasonable and dangerous. In self-defense. That is something you never learned."

"In self-defense?" Dillon's cold eyes rested on the handsome benevolent face of his chief. "You mean a man like Tom MacNeill who never lifted a hand against you or made a threat but sure was unreasonable in hanging on to his mine when you wanted it?"

"That's no way to talk. The vein he and his partners were working apexed in the Molly Green. I warned them time and again to stop working it. I even offered to buy them out."

"They had hit what figures to be a bonanza and you offer a measly thousand dollars for it. Get me right. Grab it if you like, bluff to others that it is rightly yours, but don't pull on me your holier-than-thou stuff. I'm your guntoter and I'll see nobody gets you but I don't have to believe you are any better than I am."

Johnston shook his head reproachfully. "You are a rough-talking wild ass of the desert, Black, but I know you don't mean half of what you say. Will you tell Dolph to have Burns sent to me?"

Randy came into the office with the jaunty devil-may-care manner that irked his employer. With the exception of Dillon the colonel was used to getting a subdued respect from the men he hired. He liked to meet them with pleasant condescension, to play the part of an affable, kindly superior. Even Calhoun Ives who was the most independent man in the colonel's organization had never departed from the accepted procedure.

"You sent for me?" Randy asked.

"Yes." Johnston did not ask him to sit down. "I am sending you on a mission that demands complete secrecy. Can I trust you?"

Randy drew up a chair and sat down. "I'm no blabbermouth, Colonel," he said. "A man

143

in my line plays a lone hand and listens but doesn't talk."

"That is what I want. You know that I have many enemies. A man cannot succeed as I have done without being surrounded by envy and greed and jealousy. I want you to go to Three Cedars. You will carry a letter to the superintendent of my mine and he will give you some easy job to account for your presence but you will not take him into your confidence. Two scoundrels are high-grading my ore by using a shaft adjoining the Molly Green. They had a partner, a turbulent fellow named MacNeill who went to White Rocks, got into trouble, and was killed. These men, Campbell and Scanlan, have taken it into their heads to blame me for this man's death and they are threatening my life. Previously I had tried to buy them out but they would not sell their claim though it has nothing more than a nuisance value."

Randy asked with callous indifference, "You want them taken care of?"

"No. Not yet. At least not until my safety demands it. By some means make friends with them and gain their confidence. Find out how they plan to kill me. Learn all you can about their habits. If necessary we will move first."

"Kill them, you mean?"

144

"It may come to that but I hope not," Johnston said with proper regret. "If so, they will have brought it on themselves."

"Let me get this straight, Colonel." The eyes of MacNeill, bleak and cold, searched the face of the banker. "I don't want to make a mistake. If I find out these men are dangerous, do you or don't you want me to bump them off while I am at the mine?"

Johnston thought that over before he answered. "Feel them out. Maybe they will decide to take my offer. I would rather have it that way."

"Suit yourself," Randy drawled.

"I would not kill anybody except to save my own life," the banker explained gravely. "Be discreet and don't let these men know you are working for me personally."

He offered Randy expense money. Randy declined it. He still had money of his own, he said. Later, if he had to settle the hash of these fellows the colonel could pay him what was coming in a lump sum. "And it will be plenty," he added. "I'm no cheap skate."

Outside the bank Randy rolled and lit a cigarette, took three puffs, and threw it away. Doctor Edgar and his daughter were coming up the street toward him. Polly was carrying her schoolbooks in a strap and she was talking to her father with shining eyes. They were discussing what to buy her mother for a birthday present.

Randy felt the charm of her adolescence. There was something of the fawn in her shy delicacy as if the mists of childhood lingered with her. What did a kid like Polly think about things? Despite her innocence her thoughts must be adventuring diffidently into the enigma of sex. Since his boyhood Randy had lived in a man's world and knew little about sheltered girls. This one seemed to him precious, someone apart from the harsh scene in which he had become involved.

A flag of color fluttered in her cheeks. She happened to remember that he had seen her long legs flying in a handspring and no doubt decided that she was a hoyden. Schoolboys and older men she had met but nobody like this young cowboy with the lean whipcord body and the brown face that could smile so gaily. Her thoughts had touched on him often in the past weeks.

Randy mentioned that he would be out of town for a few days but expected to return soon.

"Is it trouble again?" the doctor asked in a low voice.

"I hope not. I am trying to avoid that," Randy replied.

"If you do not leave immediately you might

drop in and call on us tonight."

"I'll be knocking on your door after supper," the young man told him, greatly pleased.

"How is your friend getting along, the one you rescued?" Polly asked.

Doctor Edgar interposed. "Mr. Burns does not like to talk about that, my dear," he said gently.

"I'm sorry," Polly cried. "I didn't know. I thought — he was getting better. You said he was, Father."

"Can Miss Polly keep a secret, Doctor?" Randy asked.

"We have always trusted her," Edgar answered.

Randy told the girl that he had taken Tom MacNeill from White Rocks secretly at night to keep him safe while he was still ill. They had moved him in a coffin. The word had got out of his death later and the report had not been contradicted. Only Mrs. Gregory in White Rocks knew he was alive.

"I won't say a word about it," Polly promised. "Cross my heart." She looked at Randy starry-eyed, happy to be taken into his confidence. Though neither of them knew it, she was enduring the joys and pains of puppy love.

As it chanced he did not keep his promise to call on the Edgars that evening. He met Ingrid Carlson near the upper end of Trail Street coming out of a cobbler's shop. In spite of the heat of the day she looked trim and cool. Busy with opening her parasol she did not shake hands.

He told her how glad he was to see her and that Tom had sent a message of thanks for all her kindness.

"He could have sent it by mail," she said coldly.

Her voice chilled him like a plunge into icy water. But he appeared not to notice this and mentioned that he had been invited to call that evening by her uncle.

She said, "I think I had better have a talk with you."

They crossed the street to the grove beside the creek.

"I see I am in the doghouse," he said.

Ingrid ignored that. "It is none of my business that you came back here to make trouble. If that is what you want you can try to be a notorious killer like that dreadful Black Dillon. I am not trying to prevent you. Please understand that."

"You are thinking of that affair at the Wagon Wheel," he protested. "I really wasn't to blame for that. Somebody had to stop that fool Steelman before he started a battle in which half a dozen men would have been killed."

"I am not talking of that at all, though I do not happen to agree with you about the blame. If you had not been in Tail Holt and in that gambling place with a gun in your hand you would not have been involved. That doesn't concern me. But something else does. I have heard twice today that you have hired yourself to Colonel Johnston as a gunman. If that is true you have no right to call at my uncle's house."

Her eyes challenged him. She wanted a denial and he could not give it. That she was right he realized. A day of reckoning was bound to come and it was not fair to involve Doctor Edgar in it, although he realized it might be too late already. He must break off any friendship between them, even though it hurt more than anything else he had ever done.

"You are right," he agreed. "Will you tell your uncle that I will not call this evening?"

"You admit that you are in this scoundrel's employ?" Ingrid demanded.

"Yes," Randy said.

"Though he did his best to murder your brother?"

"Because he tried to murder Tom." Randy lifted his hand in a gesture of appeal to her. "Can't you trust me just a little? Must you think me a blackhearted scoundrel?"

149

She was standing tall and stiff in judgment as a young Portia but he thought her eyes softened at his words. Or was it his imagination because he wanted so much for her to understand?

"No need to be dramatic," she said. "I heard a freighter today call another man a jugheaded chump. I think that fits you."

"If I am that, it is what I have to be. You know why I am here."

"Don't be foolish, Randy. There's an old saying that a man can't carry water on both shoulders. Give it up and leave here." The girl added, with a sudden impulsive warmth as if his safety was very dear to her, "Before these evil men kill you."

"I am in no danger as long as they don't know who I am," he said.

"But they will find out," she cried. "Remember what they did to Tom, how closely he shaved death."

"We have to know if we can what their plans are. Already I have some information."

"Can't you see that the more you find out the greater danger you are in? And can't you realize how Tom will feel if they — they kill you?"

She had said that what he did was of no interest to her but the urgency in the low timbre of her voice denied this. It set his pulses strumming. She was his friend even though she probably thought him a reckless fool. He was Tom's brother. No doubt that had weight with her. She was probably worrying about Tom's feelings, Randy thought, and not about him at all.

He said, with finality, "It has to be this way, Ingrid."

The girl left him with a gesture of angry impatience. He watched her go, more unhappy than he had ever been in his life, but no matter what she thought of him it was just as he had told her. It had to be this way.

Chapter Nineteen

Later that day after Ingrid Carlson had walked away from him leaving no doubt of her disapproval, Randy learned that his alliance with the Johnston group had been widely whispered through the town. When he went to the Elephant Corral to saddle his horse Cotting answered his "Hiya, Limpy" stiffly. All the old-timer's friendliness had gone. While Randy saddled he sat on the step in front of the office and ignored him.

Miserably Randy settled the bill. He liked the old codger. There had been between them a tie of mutual understanding. This was almost as bad as his parting with Ingrid.

"I'll be back in a week or so, Limpy," he said.

The faded eyes of the corral owner showed a flare of resentment. "I'll have my stalls full then," he answered. "You can go to Sugg's livery stable."

"Sore at me, Limpy?"

"Put it that I don't want your trade."

"I'm sorry," Randy said. Though he knew he could give no explanation that would satisfy Cotting, he did not want to leave without making a try. "Maybe you'll see this clearer some day."

"I've been told three times today that you have hired your gun to Johnston," the old man snapped. "Can you tell me that ain't true?"

Randy shook his head. "No, I can't tell you that, Limpy."

In Cotting's voice was an edge of scorn. His high-pitched voice flung out the last word of degradation for a cowboy. "You've done sold your saddle."

He turned on his heel and walked into the office.

Randy stood for a long minute, his arm resting on the hull of the saddle. He had to

152

make a decision. Presently he followed Cotting into the shack.

"I'm going to trust you, Limpy. I'll come clean. I need your help."

He told the old corral keeper why he had come back to town and joined up with Johnston. Eyes bright with interest and breathing hard with excitement, Cotting listened to the story.

"You blamed son of a gun," he said in a hushed voice warm with admiration. "I might of knowed it. Whyfor then are you leaving?"

"Orders from the boss," Randy chuckled. "I'm to go up to Three Cedars and get thick with those scalawags Campbell and Scanlan. I'm to find out if, when, and how they aim to bump off Johnston. If I do my work good I'll get the job of rubbing them out later."

Cotting gave a restrained whoop of mirth. "Kid, you take the cake. I never saw the beat of you." His laughter came to an abrupt halt. "But when Johnston finds out what you're up to, his gunslingers will get you certain."

"I don't think so. Not if I get wise in time to light out. Or maybe I'll get them, Limpy. This has got to be finished sometime or that scoundrel will go right on ruining good men like he has been. Men like Doctor Edgar who don't happen to cotton to the colonel's ways. Anyhow, I'll keep my eyes peeled." Randy brushed Cotting's fears aside and explained to his friend how he could help in the campaign.

Limpy jumped at the chance. There would be some risk but he was delighted to forget his years and aid in anything that would annoy Johnston. It made life worth living again. Then he added, "I think you hit on a good notion, son. One thing the colonel ain't going to die from and that's bravery. You'll have him so boogery he'll jump right out of his skin."

Randy grinned. "That is just what I'm figuring on, Limpy."

On his way to Three Cedars Randy took a detour that included White Rocks. Since he did not want to go into the town until after dark he unsaddled in a small grove of live oaks near the entrance to an arroyo. From the trees hung heavy growths of mistletoe, parasites reminding him of the riffraff gamblers and gunmen infesting all frontier towns. He dropped off to sleep and woke up to find darkness enfolding the land.

He did not ride into White Rocks by the main street but through a pasture that ran back of Mother Gregory's little hotel. It was still too early to get into touch with her, since he did not want to be recognized. After turning his mount loose to graze he waited by the back fence of her yard. The sound of a fiddle and the shuffling of dancing feet came to him from the Good Cheer saloon. A cowboy's "Hi-yi-yippy-yi!" lifted into the night. The town was beginning to wake up.

Supper was over at the Trail End House. Through the kitchen window Randy could see Mother Gregory moving to and fro putting food away. A Mexican girl was at the sink washing dishes. Presently Mrs. Gregory came into the back yard to the well. She was carrying a small pail. From the well she drew up a rope with a hook on the end of it. When she lowered it again the pail was attached to the hook. She had no ice and this was her method of keeping the butter cool.

She turned to go back into the house and found Randy at her side.

"Good gracious," she exclaimed, startled to find him there.

He drew her back into the deeper darkness behind an apple tree.

"What are you doing here?" she asked. "And why all the hush-hush?"

"I keep dreamin' about your peach pies," he drawled with a flash of white teeth in the smiling brown face. "Couldn't keep away. Maybe I'll have to marry you to get them."

"Oh, behave yourself," she laughed. He was one of her favorites and she understood

155

his nonsense. "Have you come to get into more trouble?"

"Honest, Mother, I'd ride forty miles for one of your good meals." His arm slipped around her shoulders and tightened in a hug. She was plump and short, and her face showed no beauty except that of kindness, but many a rough young fellow called her Mother and would have sold his saddle to pay any debt he owed her.

"Only you didn't, you young scamp," she told him. "You are up to some mischief."

"No mischief," he objected. "One thing I want to know. Has there been any talk that Tom is still alive?"

"I haven't heard any. I don't see how there could be. Doctor Edgar certified his death. It was announced in the *Sentinel*. You took him out of here at night in that awful coffin."

"Good. I just wanted to be sure there had been no rumors. One thing more. I want to see Jim Eliot, but I can't show myself here. Do you think you could get word to Jim to meet me back here in the pasture?"

"Yes. I'll see him myself. But you're hatching something. What is it?"

"How can you so misjudge me?" he said reproachfully. "All I want of Eliot is to do a little printing job for me. But it is very important that nobody finds out I am here or have been here. Be sure nobody hears you asking Eliot to meet me."

Mrs. Gregory said, "You crazy galoot. No more sense than a chicken floppin' around with its head cut off."

"Yes ma'am," he agreed meekly. "A sure enough nuisance."

She looked at him fondly, a young man gay and fearless and strong. Her only son she had lost when he was fourteen. If he had lived he might have been like this cowboy. Randy was not a run-of-the-range vaquero. There was a quality in him that was different. His voice, for instance, gently modulated but clear with a touch of deference for her. The lean clean look of him. He would do to take along, if one used the Western phrase that denoted complete approval.

She kissed him softly on the cheek. "Take care of yourself, son, or those scoundrels who tried to murder Tom will get you," she told him, and disappeared into the house.

It was an hour later that Randy, sitting in the chaparral close to his horse, heard the sounds of something moving through the brush.

A voice said, "Where the hell are you, MacNeill?"

Randy stepped into the open. "Think of meeting you here, Mr. Eliot," he said cheerfully. "Hope you didn't come to rustle one of

Mother Gregory's chickens."

"You know why I came, you young scamp, dragging me up here at this time of night when you can't see your hand before your face and making me stump my toes on every rock between here and Main Street," Eliot answered. "Now what do you want with me?" He was wearing his unpressed seersucker suit and a hat that had seen better years. There was no annoyance on his homely wrinkled face.

"It isn't as dark as you're letting on, Mr. Eliot," Randy replied. "You probably didn't stump your toes on more than half the rocks between here and Main Street."

"Well, what is it you want?"

"I'm a customer," Randy answered. "Rode forty miles to give you a job."

"Hmp! What kind of a job?" the editor demanded suspiciously.

"I want a poster printed and a hundred copies of it run off."

"Too lazy to come to my office or house, eh?"

Randy explained that he must not be seen and nobody must know Eliot had done the job. For his own sake he must keep it a secret. The job must be done at night.

"What you want said on this gosh-awful secret poster?" Eliot asked.

"Just a couple of lines of a song:

The dirty little coward
Who shot Johnny Howard,
They have laid Jesse James in the grave."

Eliot had heard the rumor that these words had been on Tom MacNeill's tongue when he was shot. Eliot thought about it for a long minute before he said with deep concern, "I don't get this, Randy. Are you declaring war on Johnston and his killers?"

"A defensive war," Randy answered. He explained that Johnston, in spite of his aggressive arrogance, was a very timid man who hid behind hirelings like Black Dillon and Dolph Metzger and Calhoun Ives. The words had been used against him twice and he had got the wind up. A friend in Tail Holt was going to nail the posters up in the night for Johnston to see the next morning.

"Just what do you think you will accomplish by all this?" Eliot asked.

"I am not sure," Randy confessed. "But Johnston's grip on this country must be broken or Tom can never come back and know he is safe. If I took Campbell and Scanlan back to Tail Holt with me there would be a lot of shooting and some good men would be killed. So I thought that if we could get the

159

colonel jumpy enough he might make a serious mistake."

"He might at that," Eliot said thoughtfully. "Men like Johnston are often cowards if you can get them away from their hired guns like Black Dillon. All right, I'll print the posters. You'll keep mum about it of course. How do I get them to your friend?" Eliot added a caution. "Some way so they can't be traced to me."

"Tom's blanket roll is still at Mother Gregory's. I'll get her to put the bills in it and send the roll by stage to my friend."

Before Randy left White Rocks he arranged this with Mrs. Gregory.

Chapter Twenty

Flint Morse, superintendent of the Molly Green mine, was bawling out a teamster with crackling oaths when the man who called himself Lloyd Burns came into the office. Morse held the note from Colonel Johnston in his hand but did not stop to read it until he was through blistering the mule skinner.

Randy scanned closely this slave driver who was to be his new boss. He saw a huge bulk of a man in his middle forties, bull-necked, with a salient jaw that could clamp tight as a bear trap. His two hundred and twenty pounds did not carry an ounce of fat, though the red veins in his broken-nosed face suggested that he was a heavy drinker.

Morse read the short letter from Colonel Johnston twice, scowling at it. He did not like the content. This young fellow was to be given a light job, not underground, and he was to have whatever time off he wanted, also to be given entire freedom of inspection.

"So you are a pet of the old man," the miner sneered.

"Not exactly," Randy corrected. "He thinks that after I have looked the property over I might want to put some money in it."

"You don't need to go on the pay roll for that."

"I'm a cautious guy," Randy said. "I would like to live at the company boardinghouse, be free to talk with the men as one of them, and get a chance to go down and see the vein structure whenever I like."

"All right, but you'd better not forget one thing. I'm the boss. When you want to go down ask me." Morse turned his back on him and walked out of the office.

Randy ate at the long boardinghouse table with the men. The food was good and plentiful. During the meal the miners had no time for talk. They devoted their attention to shoveling in meat, potatoes, and beans.

After supper Randy strolled over the camp. Its site made an ugly scar on a shelf plateau cut by nature into the side of a high hill. Except the shaft house all the buildings were of flimsy construction slapped together hastily. The lodes of pay ore might play out any time.

Randy asked a half-grown boy if he could tell him where Ben Scanlan lived.

"Sure," the lad answered, and pointed out a shack near the end of the crooked street.

Across the window a gunny sack had been nailed to prevent anybody from looking in. Answering Randy's knock, a voice demanded who was there.

"Could you lend a poor starving guy two bits to pay for a meal?" the man outside pleaded.

He could hear Red Campbell's excited yelp. The heavy bolt was dragged back and the door opened. "Randy MacNeill!" the redhead cried. "Where in blazes did you come from and what are you doing here?"

"Known in Tail Holt and Three Cedars as Lloyd Burns," Randy corrected. "My boss sent me here to look you two gents over. He hasn't quite made up his mind when the best time is to pump lead into you, but he'll get around to it because he figures you are too dangerous to go on living."

"Your boss?" Scanlan asked.

Randy stepped in and the door was bolted again. "Gent by the name of Johnston. Calls himself colonel, but nobody knows how and when he got to be one. Story is that he hired a substitute to fight for him during the war."

"Sure, we have heard all that," Scanlan said impatiently, "but what's that got to do with you?"

Randy grinned. "I'm one of his rattlesnake stompers."

Scanlan said, "You're loadin' us."

"Cross my heart," Randy insisted, mirth in his dancing eyes. "I reckon pretty soon I'll have to do my stompin' on you two."

"Wait a minute," Red cut in. "Fellow just up from Tail Holt was telling me about a boy who had a difficulty with the Butch Halloran gang when they came in to shoot up the Wagon Wheel. Seems he was a stranger. Couldn't of been you?"

"No difficulty," Randy answered. "Steelman got on the prod and I winged him. That ended the trouble. So Johnston decided with a little urging that he could use me."

They made him tell the whole story of his adventure since he arrived at Tail Holt. When he had finished they flung questions at him.

Their interest centered particularly in Johnston's gunmen. He mentioned Black Dillon, Dolph Metzger, and the croupier Ives. There were several more whom he suspected were employed partly at least on account of their proficiency with a pistol but he was not certain of this.

"Dillon is with Johnston almost all the time," Randy explained. "He's a back-shooting scoundrel if I ever saw one. Metzger's a bad one, too. We'd know that from the way he treated Tom. I would call him a smiling back-slapping hypocrite. I am not so sure about Calhoun Ives. Around Tail Holt he has a reputation for being honest."

"You are dead sure he does not know who you are?" Scanlan asked anxiously. "He might be leading you up an alley."

Randy shook his head. "No. Johnston is very timid. That is surprising for a man with the reputation he has, but he dived for cover behind the piano in the Wagon Wheel when the Halloran gang showed up. If he did not think I was just a cold-blooded triggerman he wouldn't let me near him."

"So you think we are safe for another week or two," Red said.

"Yes. He made it plain to me. The people at Tail Holt hate him. Some of them think he ordered Tom's death — as he did — and they are full of suppressed anger. He does not dare wipe you out so soon. When he does try I feel sure he will hope to make it look like an accident."

"He could do that by having somebody set a charge at the face of the tunnel where we are working," Scanlan said.

"We had better sleep in the shaft house and see that nobody has a chance to get down," Red proposed.

"Good idea," Randy agreed. "I am going to act mad at you when I go back to town so that he will give me the job of looking after you birds."

They discussed their mine. Both of Randy's partners were enthusiastic about it. They were in pay ore and had blocked out enough to feel sure the vein was not just a pocket. But from the breast where they were working they could hear the blasts of a Molly Green crew and they were convinced the men were opening a drift belonging to the three partners.

"Flint Morse claims our Argonaut lode has its apex in Molly Green territory," Scanlan said. "You know that, of course, and you also know it is a lie. If Johnston sues to evict us he will be beat, so he does the only other thing he can. He orders us to get off the earth or get killed."

"It gripes him to think he could have filed on this claim and struck a bonanza instead of on the Molly Green where the fissure vein is peterin' out," Red explained. "Kid, we've got it and he hasn't. That's the size of it. Point is, can we hold it?"

"We'll hold it," Scanlan said grimly. "What I'm thinking is that even after he is well Tom can't come back as long as Johnston is alive, and Red and me ain't safe either. We will have to get Johnston or he will get us."

"I can warn you when he gets ready to move," Randy said.

"If you are still alive." Scanlan shook his head. "I don't like the game you're playing. It is loaded with dynamite. And what could we do if you did warn us? Go hide in a barrel somewhere?"

"If you have an idea," Campbell said, "let's hear it."

"I was thinking about the Halloran gang," Scanlan said. "If half of what we hear is true, Butch Halloran would like nothing better than to clean out the whole Johnston outfit. We would be doing the people of the territory a favor if we got Halloran to do it."

"You will have to leave the Halloran bunch out of it," Randy said firmly.

"Why?" Scanlan demanded.

"They would come into town shooting," Randy explained. "They would probably burn it and kill people who had nothing to do with

Johnston and his ruffians. This is our job and we will have to handle it in our own way when the sign is right."

"And meanwhile we go hide in the closet," Scanlan grumbled.

Campbell did not like the idea of waiting and hiding any better than his partner, but he saw sense in what Randy had said. He looked at the tall, lithe cowboy, and he decided that young as he was, Randy could be counted on when the chips were down.

"He's right, Ben," Campbell said. "We can take care of ourselves without asking the Hallorans for help."

"Has Flint Morse bothered you since we last met?" Randy asked.

"He has worked on our men and two have quit," Scanlan answered glumly. "He has fixed it so it's hard for us to hire good men. When one of us meets Morse he talks ugly. He is spoiling for a fight. I've heard he has never been licked in a fist brawl."

"I've taken his rough tongue twice," Red said. "Next time he will have to show me."

Randy's gaze took in the heavily packed shoulders of Red and the bulging muscles of his arms. He must be nearly forty but there was a youthful jauntiness in the way he carried himself. Very likely he could put up a good fight but Flint Morse weighed thirty pounds more than he did. If they ever tangled, Red would probably take a terrible beating.

Chapter Twenty-one

On his way out after breakfast from the house where the men ate, Flint Morse stopped opposite Randy to fling an accusation at him. "You went down last night and spent an hour with those fellows who are stealing our ore."

"Maybe we had better talk this over alone, Mr. Morse," the young man suggested.

"Nothing to talk over. I'll let Colonel Johnston know that the fellow he sent up here to be coddled is thick as thieves with his enemies."

"Look at it my way, Mr. Morse. If I am going to invest in the Molly Green I want to know what right those men have to be working so close to us they are almost breathing down our necks. So I asked them."

"I could have told you," the mine superintendent said harshly. "No right at all." He added with a malicious grin, "Since you are to get a nice soft job where you won't be in danger I'll give you one. You can go to work as

168

flunky for the cook. No chance of you getting hurt washing dishes."

If Randy felt the needle he did not show it. "Good of you to be so thoughtful for me," he said.

The cook already had a seventeen-year-old boy for a flunky but he told Randy he could saw wood for the cookstove. The underground men carried dinner pails with them but when the gong sounded for those above, Randy dropped his ax to join them for the meal. He had sawed and chopped a pile that would last for several days.

He decided to inspect the stopes that afternoon. Morse accompanied him ungraciously, but he showed his unwelcome guest all he wanted to see. At the face of one drift they could hear the dull sound of men working in the Argonaut.

As they entered the cage to ascend to the surface Morse flung an angry question at Randy. "What the hell are you doing here anyhow? Has Johnston sent you here to spy on me?"

"No. But guess again. I can't tell you any more."

"So that's it. Well, go back and tell the boss I can take care of these gents without any help from you."

"I have to obey the orders given me. Fact

is, he wants to let things run along the way they are for a while. Any trouble right now might raise a rookus he can't afford."

"Yeah, he's like that," Morse said scornfully. "No guts to carry through. Always wants to cover up."

"He had that Tom MacNeill bumped off," Randy mentioned.

"If he hadn't a yellow streak he would of fixed it to have all three of them knocked out at once. A damned cowardly killing, I call it."

Randy agreed with a nod. If Morse had not been a bold ruffian he would not have spoken so plainly. With encouragement he might go farther. What he had said greatly surprised MacNeill.

"Yeah, the colonel is a cautious duck," the younger man agreed. "He wants dead certainties — sent three men to kill MacNeill from cover when one could have done it. Black Dillon didn't need Metzger and Ives. Unless he figured Campbell and Scanlan might be at White Rocks with MacNeill."

Morse did not follow the lead opened. "You're too brash with names, fellow," he growled. "I guess you don't know Calhoun Ives very well. That kind of shooting is not his style. Anyhow, Johnston only sent one man."

They walked out of the shaft house to step into a heated controversy. Red Campbell had left by the roadside two drills he had been sharpening at his outdoor blacksmith shop and he claimed that a Cousin Jack working for the Molly Green had taken them.

"I'll handle this, Williams," Morse told the Welshman curtly, brushing him aside with a sweep of his great muscled arm. He moved toward Campbell with heavy-footed stride. "You can't call one of my men a thief and get away with it, you scut. You're for it."

Red unbuckled his belt and handed it to Randy. This was not going to be a gun fight. He said, "Understand, nobody butts in. This is between us and goes to a finish."

Randy knew that what Red said was meant for him. Sooner or later these two men had to clash in a battle. But he had to try to stop it. He stepped between the men.

"Let's get this straight," he said. "Did you accuse Williams of stealing the drills or taking them by mistake, Red?"

"Nobody but a fool would steal drills when his outfit has a half a ton of them," Red replied. "But he got sore when I told him they were mine. Hell, it doesn't matter anyhow. Bully Morse has been spoilin' for a fight. Now he's got one. Keep out of it, kid."

Morse came in with wide swinging loops of the right and left. He paid no attention to defense. That was the way he fought, to hammer his opponent down into a battered heap, face raw as an uncooked beefsteak and legs limp as a rag doll. But Red had been a prizefighter in his youth and hard work had kept him in perfect trim. He took the blows on his elbows and pumped in the skilled boxer's jolting one-two at the big man's exposed belly.

The superintendent grunted and charged again. One of his fists landed on the side of Red's head and flung him back against the wall of the shaft house. Campbell ducked, sidestepped, and backed away until he had shaken off the momentary dizziness.

Morse fought flatfooted, crowding his foe, pouring in slashing roundhouse drives many of which went wild. Those that landed had the jolting kick of a mule. Watching Red, Randy was surprised at his shifty footwork. He was a moving target, warding off most of the punishment with arms, shoulders, and jarring counters.

Out of breath, Morse stopped for a moment, glaring at his elusive opponent. "Come on and fight, damn you, and stop dancing around," he snarled.

His face was unmarked, but his breath was coming heavily. All of Red's attack had been at the man's vulnerable body. Morse was a heavy drinker. His great strength he still had but not the wind for a long battle. Though he had cut and badly bruised Campbell's face, it came to him with the shock of a surprise that unless he could stop the savage blows pounding at his midriff he would be beaten. Already he had to gulp for air and his heavy limbs were tiring.

Red got inside the flailing windmills and hammered a left to the kidneys and a right to the chin. Morse closed, taking a sharp uppercut, one arm encircling his enemy's waist and the fingers of the other trying to gouge Campbell's eyes. Red kneed him. They went to the ground together, rolling one over the other, each spreading his legs for a leverage to hold his enemy down.

Red broke free and was on his feet while Morse's fingers were still pushing him up from the road. He smashed pile-driving fists at the unprotected head of the mine superintendent. Morse came up, his face raw and bleeding, and by sheer weight drove Red to the wall again, disregarding the sharp jabs battering his eyes and cheeks and pounding at the ribs of the redhead. With all the strength in him Red's clenched hand landed an uppercut beneath the jaw of Morse, who staggered back, the huge body sagging, the arms falling to his sides lax and loose.

Before he could recover, Red was on him. His slogging fists landed on the big man's mauled face a dozen times until the mashed lips, the bleeding cheeks, and the glassy eyes gave it the appearance of a gargoyle. At last the swaying body went down heavily and lay motionless.

Red leaned against the wall completely exhausted, one eye closing shut, his cheeks bruised and bleeding.

"If I hadn't seen it I wouldn't have believed any man alive could have done that to Flint Morse," a miner said.

"Maybe Mr. Morse won't be so free with his dukes after this," a Welsh miner added with deep satisfaction. He had felt the weight of the superintendent's hard fists more than once.

Randy said happily, "Mr. Morse chose the wrong man this time."

"I might have been mistaken about the drills," Williams said glumly. "I'll put them back where I picked them up."

Randy walked with his partner to the shack where the battered man lived. He brought a bucket of water from the small mountain stream which leaped down from the slope above on its way to the plain. Red stripped to the waist and washed his wounds. Though his ribs were sore from the slamming fists of Morse, the man's main attack had been at the bobbing weaving red head of the ex-prizefighter. Red's face was badly cut and bruised.

"I thought he had me once or twice," Red said. "That right of his is like the pounding of a pile driver."

"He'll never forgive you," Randy told his friend. "You have hurt his pride terribly. He'll stop your clock certain if he can."

Randy spent the night with his partners at the cabin. Scanlan was of opinion that the fight was likely to bring to issue quicker an attempt to get rid of them. It would be like Morse to take action without waiting for orders from Johnston. With this opinion Randy disagreed but they decided never to leave the house without being armed.

Scanlan was despondent about the situation. They were like sitting ducks waiting to be shot. He could not see how the kid had done any good getting in with Johnston. The old devil was still after their scalps and he would keep on unless they got his, but he did not mention the Hallorans again. He was satisfied to grumble that he would be better off as a live man but poor than a dead one who had once owned a share in a bonanza.

The others knew he was more or less right but they were aware he did not want to throw in his hand any more than they did.

Chapter Twenty-two

Randy MacNeill was eating dinner at the boardinghouse when the dull roar of the explosion sounded. None of those at the table needed to be told that an accident in the mine had occurred. Randy rose with the others and hurried to the scene.

Four wild-eyed men came out of the Molly Green shaft house. They had just reached the surface from below. The roof of a tunnel had collapsed and buried five miners in the drift where they had been working. A tremendous mass of rock and dirt had crashed down from the level above and cut the miners off from the exit. They were buried alive.

Within a few minutes everybody in Three Cedars had gathered at the scene, among them wailing wives and children of the trapped men. Since the previous day Morse had not left his room. Food had been carried to him. He could not bring himself to face those who were gloating at his humiliation. But he was among the first to reach the shaft mouth and he set efficiently about the work of rescue. A space was roped off to hold back the crowd. He gave orders for men to get ready for rescue work, then had himself lowered into the mine to examine the situation himself.

Randy felt a touch on his shoulder and turned to see Red.

"They are caught in the drift Morse has been opening toward us," he said. "I don't know how big the block-up of the tunnel is, but we'll know when Morse comes up. Maybe the best way to get at the men if they are alive is from the face where we are drilling."

"You were underground when the rock gave way," Randy said. "Afterward did you hear any sign that the men are alive?"

"No, but they may be. I didn't wait but came right up."

When Morse stepped out of the cage he reported that the fallen rock filled the tunnel for many yards. He organized teams to take turns at drilling and sent the first one down equipped with picks, shovels, hammers, powder, fuse and caps. He would join them presently as soon as he had set the men above to sharpening drills and the women to preparing coffee and food for those fighting to free the miners caught behind twenty tons of broken rock.

Randy approached him and said he had a plan to offer.

"Damn your plans," Morse told him impatiently. "I have to save lives and no time to waste."

"It won't take you a minute to listen," Randy urged. "I've been down into the Argonaut. The face of the drift where Campbell and Scanlan are working is close to where your men are trapped. I could hear clearly the sound of their drilling. The Argonaut men are in hard rock with no danger of the roof caving in, but in your tunnel every tram load you cart away makes greater the chance of another cave-in."

Morse caught his point instantly. This brash young fool might be right. It would be safer to blast through hard rock than to risk starting another slide from the weakened level above. In mucking out the debris that would be a constant danger.

"I'll have a look," he said, and started for the shaft house of the Argonaut.

Red Campbell went down with him in the cage and led the way to the breast. Morse showed no sign of recognizing his presence.

"My guess is that we are four or five feet higher than where the Molly Green men are," Red explained. "We'll have to slant down to them."

Morse picked up bits of broken quartz left on the floor after the last blast. They were hard and firm with no sign of crumbling at the edges.

"I'll send a shift down," Morse said. "We'll work entirely from here."

"Our men will take the first shift," Red replied with decision. "Get down to us water and sharp drills."

"They're my men," Morse retorted, glaring at him.

"This is our mine — yet," Red countered sharply.

There came to them from the other side of the rock breast the sound of a tapping hammer.

"Glory be, they're alive," Red cried, and beat a reply on the wall with the blunt end of a drill. He gave a curt order to Morse. "Send our three men down, and Scanlan. Lend us two of yours for muckers. We'll work two-hour shifts, then let yours take over for the next two."

Morse turned and left without a word. His duty was to get his imprisoned men out safely. Until then his quarrel with these two could wait.

Red picked up a drill and slipped it into a hole one of his men had started before the accident. Randy held it steady while Red swung the hammer on the blunt end. The ringing of the steel fell rhythmically stroke after stroke.

When the drills bit into the wall to nearly their full length a longer one was substituted. Still Red swung the hammer, his heavy shoulder muscles giving each blow force. Candles stuck into the side walls threw out enough light to see. At the end of each swing the steel struck the drill head true. A longer drill and still a longer tore into the rock. Giant-powder and fuse were tamped in and the charge fired.

The men hurried back into the tunnel end, the air heavy with poisonous fumes. Muckers grew busy wheeling away the broken slabs while others attacked the face with new sharpened drills. Reliefs were frequent to let those below get into the clean air outside and rest their weary muscles.

There had been one shot from the side of the trapped men but only one. Randy guessed that they dare not foul up more the limited air supply. They had to trust to their comrades to reach them before it was exhausted.

The Molly Green was shorthanded and Morse saw to it that every man did his bit. There was no need to pressure them, for all were desperately anxious to save the imprisoned men. Friend and foe worked side by side. Morse followed Red, discussed with him the angle of dip to take. The wall in front of them was the only enemy and they slogged at it with mighty blows, each refusing to give place to lesser men as long as he could swing the hammer without endangering the holder.

Randy was one of the muckers. His task was to drag from the breast the rock torn from the wall face by the heavily loaded shots. The foul smoke and fumes sickened him. He would not give up, though his legs were rubbery and his breath came raggedly. He stumbled over a spur of quartz projecting from the floor and fell heavily, as down and out as a prizefighter who is dropped by a Sunday punch.

When Randy came to he was being lifted from the cage into the sweet pure air of a sunny morning. Like the others, he was naked to the waist, his body soiled with sweat and blackened with dirt. Every muscle ached. He had never known such weariness. In half an hour he was back again in the tunnel.

The day wore away and night fell, but the weary arms still swung hammers and pushed the wheelbarrows, and sharpened drills for the attack. The shifts were shorter now, for human endurance was wearing down. But they were drawing nearer to the end of the granite wall.

"Listen," Morse cried out suddenly to Red Campbell.

They could hear the sound of picks from the prison. The rock was getting softer. They could no longer set off shots lest tons of brecciated rock pour down on rescuers and prisoned men alike. Hammers and drills were flung aside and picks taken up. Dogged, grim, and haggard, the sappers held to their task. Men reeled back to the foot of the shaft and lay there spent, gasping for breath. Others moved in to take their place. The endless hours dragged on through the night to another day.

The wall in front of them had narrowed down to less than two feet. For the last few yards they had timbered as they went, wedging their sets against the walls and the crumbling roof.

Morse and Red were at the face with their picks and Randy behind them removing the rubbish as it fell. All the other men underground had been ordered back to the shaft by Morse. The danger of another cave-in was apparent. The rumble of small slides on both sides of the narrowing barrier was increasing. The least disturbance might release many tons of shale and disintegrated quartz on them.

The superintendent shouted for the men beyond the wall to stop work. He and Red handled the picks with great care. Loosened slabs they picked from the breast with their bare hands. A flame of light showed in the wall from one pick thrust.

Somebody inside, unable to wait, was tearing at the barrier with a shovel.

"Let be before you bring the whole thing down on us," Morse ordered.

The opening grew larger. Another small slide filled it. Red scooped the rubble out with his stiff fingers while Morse tapped with small strokes of the pick. He clawed out a large slab of flat rock. One of the men inside gave out a feeble cheer. He could see daylight now.

"Are you all alive?" Morse asked.

"Just," a raw voice croaked. "Happen you had been an hour later none of us would have lasted."

"Any of you hurt?"

"Two. For God's sake get us out of this hell hole."

Red dropped his pick, staggered back to the side of the tunnel, and slid down. He had reached the limit of endurance. Morse enlarged the opening.

"I'm smaller than you," Randy told Morse. "I'd better go in and help them out."

One man wiggled his way out of the cavern. "Do the hurt men need help?" Morse asked.

"Mike has a broken leg and Bill's shoulder is badly smashed," the miner told him.

Randy worked carefully through the gap, trying not to disturb the friable rock. A hollow-eyed man, moving on leaden feet, was trying to drag one of the wounded forward. He and Randy passed him out head first to Morse. The man with the broken leg went next. A miner lying on the floor pushed himself to his feet. His knee hinges gave way and Randy caught him before he fell. Chunks of rock were dropping from the roof as he was lifted and pushed out of the cavern. Randy left the prison last. The air in it was so bad he wondered how the men had kept alive. Already he was sick from drawing it into his lungs.

Red was back on his feet ready to help. The rescuers were so exhausted and the wounded such a hindrance that they moved toward the shaft scarcely faster than a crawl.

"Go get Jock and Andy to help," Morse told MacNeill.

Randy hurried to the foot of the shaft and brought three men back with him. Travel was not so slow now. They were out of the danger zone just in time. Behind them the roar of an avalanche sounded. The heavy dust swept over them so quickly that for a few moments they could not see one another. The tunnel behind them was gone.

The voice of Morse came out of the choking cloud. "All right, boys. We're in hard rock now. The roof won't cave."

In the first cage load the wounded were lifted to the surface. Those waiting below heard the cheer that went up as they were helped from the shaft house. Morse had gone with them to give orders for their care. The last to get into the lift were Red and Randy.

Scanlan met them at the surface. Unsteady from extreme exhaustion both moved like drunken men.

"Better get to the cabin and tumble into bed," Scanlan said. "I'm for sleep, too." All day and the night before he had been working at the blacksmith shop sharpening drills.

"Right," Randy agreed. "Don't waken me for a week."

A buckboard had been waiting to take the wounded to their homes. Worn out though he was, Morse was giving directions for moving them and for preparing food and coffee for the rescuers. Randy admired the masterly decision with which the man took charge. The fellow might be a bully but there was in him the tough strength for leadership.

Around a bend in the hill a buggy came, in it a man and a woman. Randy watched it, a sudden interest showing in his tired eyes.

"By golly, it's Doctor Edgar," somebody cried.

Randy followed Morse to the buggy when it stopped.

"You're just in time, Doc," the superintendent said. "We dug the boys out and brought
them up not five minutes ago. You made good
time."

"All of them alive?" the doctor asked.

"Yes. One has a broken leg and another a
crushed shoulder." He added, after a moment, "Some are feeling pretty shaky. In another hour they would all have been gone. We
can thank these boys here for saving them. It
was a hellish job."

"I have brought my niece with me," the
doctor said. "She is a nurse. Miss Carlson —
Mr. Morse. You had better get these men to
bed where we can look after them."

Ingrid rose and gathered her skirts around
her preparatory to descending from the
buggy. Randy offered her a bleeding grimy
hand to help her down. His clothes were torn
and filthy. He was naked from the waist up
and every inch of hard slim body was stained
with sweat and dirt. She guessed that he like
the others had been, until a few minutes before, facing the imminent risk of death for
hours. Yet the white teeth in his brown face
showed in a gay smile that had already ban-
ished the horror of the experience.

Without a moment's hesitation she took his
hand and came down lightly. The warm Scan-
dinavian color was in her cheeks. She met him

on his own terms, her face crinkling to mirth.

"Haven't we met before, Mr. — Bird?" she asked.

"Burns," he corrected. "Miss Nightingale, I believe."

Doctor Edgar nodded stiffly to Randy. He was a simple man who followed a straight undeviating line. It was his strong opinion that an honest man should have no more dealings with Johnston than circumstances forced upon him. Yet this young fellow had let himself become deeply involved in a dishonorable course. In the end it would probably destroy him. Edgar was worried about this, for in spite of his disapproval he liked Randy Mac-Neill and saw in him great possibilities.

Chapter Twenty-three

Randy flung himself on a bunk still dressed and fell into a deep sleep. When he awoke it was late afternoon of the next day. It took him a moment to remember why he was sore in every muscle.

Red Campbell had awakened half an hour earlier and was cooking breakfast. "Son," he invited, "come and get it. For you and me this is last night's supper and today's breakfast and dinner."

"My belly is as flat as an empty mail sack," Randy said.

He drew up at the table and both of them ate ravenously.

"Where is Ben?" he asked.

"Gone to get a couple of pails of water for us to wash off all this tunnel muck that's on us."

"I never want to spend a tougher twenty-four hours," the younger man said. "Most of the time I thought we'd never make it."

"Me too. When we got into the soft rock I was plumb scared. Lucky we had Morse with us. He sure held us to it."

"Some man. Without him we would never have got to the boys in time. Wish he was on our side."

Scanlan came in carrying two full water buckets.

"Doc says Mike and Bill will come through all right," he told them.

After Randy had bathed he looked ruefully at his soiled torn trousers. "I bought these two weeks ago and a rag-picker wouldn't take them now," he mourned.

But since they were all he had he wore them.

"Go heeled," Red advised as Randy headed for the door. "You never can tell."

Randy picked his belt up from the bed and buckled it around his waist. "Don't think there is any need of it," he said. "I'm still one of Johnston's sacred cows and not on the black list like you fellows."

"That's what you think," Red replied. "Johnston and his killer may have another idea."

The sun was setting in a splash of glory. The squalid street in the foreground offered an ugly contrast. Randy looked up and down it with distaste, a camp fouled by men, but the background was a picture painted by the Master Artist. The impression lingered only for a moment until he caught sight of Ingrid Carlson coming out of a miner's cabin. She moved down the road with the light tread he felt she must have inherited from her Viking ancestors.

When he caught up with her he asked how her patients were doing.

"They are beginning to take notice of me," she laughed. "That is a good sign of convalescence. One of them asked me if I was married."

He said, "I'm not sure I want you to notice me much while I look like a scarecrow."

"If you are ragged it is in a good cause." She added, knowing it would plague him, "A man told me half an hour ago that you saved his life."

"He is crazy," Randy answered, "unless he means that all the men in camp helped in the rescue work."

"Did all of them climb through that small hole into the trap where they were caught?" she asked.

"Tommyrot! It just happened that at the moment I was the smallest man near the rock face. If the cave-in had come a few minutes earlier it would have caught the others, too." He tried a little dig at her. "Did you tell him you were a poor lonesome spinster?"

"I told him I still had hope," she replied cheerfully. "Is it news to you that Dolph Metzger drove into the camp an hour ago?"

This sobered Randy but his face did not show it. The man of course had been sent by Johnston. After the accident the colonel would want to know all the information he could learn about it. That might be the sole reason for Metzger being here. Or he might have come for a more sinister purpose.

"Johnston wants a report on the explosion," he said.

"I don't like it." Ingrid's concern expressed itself in a voice sharp with rebuke. "The miners you pulled out of that hole have talked with me. They think unless Mr. Campbell and Mr. Scanlan leave at once they are doomed. You will be trapped with them."

"We are a tough outfit," he answered cheerfully. "There is no pressing danger, not if we keep a stout front. Try to understand our position, Ingrid. We are grown men. Because a ruthless scoundrel like Colonel Johnston threatens us we can't run away and leave a mine in which there is a fortune to be made. We have to stay with it and beat him, or quit calling ourselves men." Randy searched for what might be a parallel case in her life. "If a smallpox epidemic broke out in this camp would you run away like a scared rabbit?"

"Not the same," she objected. "It would be my duty to stay." She shrugged her shoulders in resignation. "You are such a stubborn fool I don't know why I like you."

"I know why I like you," he said quickly, "and I want to tell you some of the reasons. There are so many — "

She cut him off abruptly. "I was talking with Mr. Morse. He is annoyed because Colonel Johnston sent you here — thinks it may have been to spy on him. But he praised you and Mr. Campbell for helping to save his men. I'll ask him to tell the colonel what you did."

"That will be nice," Randy said, and carefully kept sarcasm out of his voice. He knew this would not make the least difference to Johnston, but it might comfort the girl to

191

think she was doing something to help.

They walked down the hill to the house of the nearest patient. At the door she urged, a worried wrinkle in her forehead, "You'll be careful, won't you?"

"I've got a reason for living a long long time," he replied. "I guess you don't want to hear about it now, but someday I will tell you anyway."

She did not tell him she wanted to hear the reason now but color ran deeper in her cheeks. When he offered a hand in goodbye she assumed surprise, but her firm clasp warmed him like wine. This beautiful girl was on his side.

Randy moved down the shabby crooked street with the light-footed step of one on top of the world. His thoughts were very pleasant and he was whistling "My Bonnie Lies Over the Ocean." He could not tell Ingrid how he felt about her until this trouble with Johnston was over, but he was sure she knew, and she would listen to him when the time came. He thought she returned his feeling or she would not be so worried about his safety.

Dolph Metzger was sitting on the steps of the Molly Green rooming-house porch. He took a long black cigar from his mouth to wave a hand at MacNeill.

"I hear you did quite a job yesterday," his

hearty voice boomed out. "Tell me about it, Burns." His smile was warm and friendly but it did not reach the cold eyes. It was the professional smile of a backslapper.

Randy took the offered hand and sat down beside the manager of the Wagon Wheel. He discounted entirely the bonhomie that was Metzger's stock-in-trade. The fellow was not only a smooth and slippery hypocrite but a dangerous killer.

"We had quite a bit of excitement but we got the boys out," Randy said.

Colonel Johnston had not told Metzger what this young fellow's mission here was. That was one of Johnston's annoying habits. He did not tell his right hand what his left hand was doing. Metzger tried fishing for information.

"The boss wants to know how you are getting along on the job," he mentioned casually.

Just a little too casually, Randy thought. He said, noncommittally, "Report I'm doing all right."

"That doesn't tell him much."

"He'll understand," Randy replied. "Tell him that Morse did a fine rescue job. Without him we would never have got through to the boys. I was one of half a dozen muckers he used as relays. We did not have it too easy, but it was Morse and that fellow Red Campbell who carried the load. One or the other of them was at the breast hammering in the drills nearly all the time. Neither of them quit as long as he could stand and swing."

"I don't get it," Metzger said. "The way I hear it they had a terrific fight the day before. Why would they be working together?"

Randy looked at the man with a cautious covered scorn. "You and I don't understand men like them. We have sold ourselves to do the devil's work, and so we have a different way of looking at things. Morse and Campbell aren't hired guns. They are free men. When those poor fellows were trapped they thought only of trying to save them."

"I hear you were down in the drift with them," Metzger said dryly. "I guess that makes you a hero, too."

"To hell with that kind of talk," Randy flung at him impatiently. "I'm here to do a job. The guys caught in that hell hole were our men. If I had sat on my prat and watched others do the job, where would I have stood with Johnston or with anybody here in the camp? I had to make a play."

"Yeah, I notice making plays is your stock in trade," Metzger said sourly. "Anything to get attention. Little Mr. Johnny-on-the-spot. That's you."

"You have an objection to that?" Randy

194

asked, his voice low and cold.

Metzger backed away from the retort to his sarcasm. He had no wish to tangle with this young devil. "No offense meant," he said hastily. "But will you tell me one thing? Why did you line up with Red Campbell in his fight with Morse?"

"I didn't exactly line up with him and I won't tell you why I did what I did. I was sent here to do a job and I will do what I have to do. If you are not satisfied with my answer take it up with Colonel Johnston. He'll probably warn you to mind your own business."

Randy rose and walked away. He hoped he had left the impression of a callous young scoundrel trying to earn the reputation of a redoubtable bad man. Not that Metzger in himself amounted to anything. Beneath his veneer of hardness the man was soft. But Black Dillon was not soft. Neither was the croupier Calhoun Ives. Nor were Morse and Campbell. In this league where Randy was playing it did not take long to separate the men from the boys. Randy had to play his role to the hilt. He would be satisfied if Metzger returned to Tail Holt and reported that Lloyd Burns was a hardcase, a good man to let alone.

Scowling, Metzger watched him move down the street, hat tiptilted and apparently carefree. He thought, *This young fool is as dan-*

gerous as Black Dillon but he is too reckless and won't live as long. And on the heel of that came another reflection, that Dillon was already jealous of Burns. With a little judicious prodding the dislike could be fanned into explosive hatred, the result of which might be that they would destroy each other, leaving the road clear for Dolph Metzger to rise to the top in Johnston's organization.

He saw Morse come out of the mess tent. The superintendent stopped for a few words with the young man and then joined Metzger.

"I've been wondering whether one of these Argonaut men could be responsible for the accident," Metzger said.

"You can forget that. None of them had a chance. In a mine those things happen."

"One thing I don't understand is why this pup Burns has been hanging around Campbell and Scanlan. He's supposed to be on our side. At least he's taking the colonel's pay."

"Your side — not mine," Morse corrected. "I'm hired to run this mine. I'll take orders from the boss about that. Nothing more."

"That wasn't how you talked last time I saw you."

"It's how I talk now."

"Beats me. You have a fight with this fellow Campbell and he whips you. Don't you want to get even with him?"

Morse flushed angrily. "I'll fight him any day at the drop of a hat and I'll beat him. But, by God, he's a man and I'm not sure you and Dillon and the rest of your bunch are. Campbell sided me in the tunnel when all hell was to pay. I'll not join in any dirty work against him and if I can help it I won't let anybody else pull any shenanigan. You go back and tell Johnston that. And you can tell him something else. I am getting damned tired of having him send men up here to spy on me."

"He won't like it."

"Then he can lump it."

"My guess is you'll lose your job."

"Maybe I'll go to work for the Argonaut."

"A pair of highgraders."

"Tell that to outsiders but not to me. I know who is right and who is wrong in this fight and I know which mine has struck pay ore and which is in *borasca*. I've made it hard for those guys but not any more." He shook a finger under Metzger's nose. "I tell you they are men. If you think you are half as good, get hold of a shovel and see how long you last mucking out behind Red Campbell."

"This doesn't sound like Bully Morse," Metzger said, puzzled. "You're supposed to be the toughest rock buster and slave driver in the West. What's got into you, man?"

"I still am if the layout's honest," Morse

197

said. "I've finally got my bellyful, that's all. I ought to have quit when Tom MacNeill was killed. Murder is one thing I have never tied in with."

"That's no way to talk, Flint," Metzger reproved. "This MacNeill goes on a wild spree, jerks out a gun, and gets bumped off. Is Colonel Johnston to blame because the young fool was a trouble hunter?"

Morse turned sullen. He thought he had talked enough, perhaps too much. What he had said would be carried to the boss and very likely he would lose his job.

"I hear talk," he said sourly. "Maybe there's nothing to it. Point is, I'm running the Molly Green. I don't like these guys who own the Argonaut, but if it comes to gun play, and it looks to me like it will, I'm on the sidelines. Don't try to drag me into your feud. I'll have no part in it. Understand?"

Metzger's face showed shocked innocence. He had come to feel Morse out as to the best way of arranging an accident in the Argonaut but that idea had to be dropped, at least as far as help from the mine manager went.

"You're away off, Flint," he said. "Any trouble with these fellows will be settled inside the law."

To Metzger it was plain that Colonel Johnston had lost ground at Three Cedars. He had talked with several miners and he could sense their changed attitude toward the men of the Argonaut. The explosion had been unfortunate in that it had wiped out any hostility between the two parties. Every man in the camp had helped to rescue the group trapped underground. With the exception of Morse the one who had done most was Campbell. Any action to injure him would be greatly resented, but Metzger wasn't sure he could make Johnston understand that.

Metzger left that afternoon to return to Tail Holt. Next day Randy got a message from Johnston recalling him.

Chapter Twenty-four

Randy MacNeill reached Tail Holt under a night of stars. He pulled up at the big billboard which announced this was Johnstown. Six posters covered the lettering and each of them carried the same legend concerning the death of Jesse James. Limpy must have nailed them up after dark not more than an hour or two ago.

As Randy passed down the business street

fronting the creek he saw men already busy ripping down the posters. He tied at the Wagon Wheel and pushed through the batwing doors. The time was two hours after midnight and the place was humming with activity.

Ives turned the wheel over to another man and joined Randy.

"Time to light a fire," he said, and put a match to a long cigar.

Randy noticed that he had moved with the lithe grace of a lazy cat. He was a Texan, always relaxed and easy, but if report was true he could jump into action lightning quick when danger threatened.

"The boss here?" Randy asked. "Just got in and thought I'd better report."

A touch of sardonic amusement lit the cold eyes of the gambler. "You're a little late. He left in a hurry ten minutes ago and took the Shadow with him. Somebody placarded this town with doggerel and he got goose quills running up and down his back, so Black took him home and tucked him in his crib."

"Doggerel?" Randy quizzed.

"That Jesse James song. Seems that Tom MacNeill was singing it when he got bumped off. The brave colonel is superstitious and figures that MacNeill's ghost has come back to haunt him. He is also scared stiff." Ives's lips curled in contempt. "We might as well admit the truth, Burns. Our boss has a broad yellow streak down his back. If he didn't have us to back him up with our guns he wouldn't amount to a damn."

"I'd better wait till tomorrow to see him," Randy suggested.

"Yeah, I guess you had. Heard you had quite a party at the mines."

Randy nodded. "Touch and go at the finish. If it hadn't been for Morse and that fellow Campbell we never would have made it."

"How come Campbell to have chips in the game?" Ives asked. "Story going around that Morse and he had a terrific fight the day before."

"That's right. I never saw a better slam-bang battle. But both of them forgot it when those five miners were trapped in the drift."

Ives nodded. He was the kind who could understand that. Men did not stand with arms folded when such an accident occurred, although Randy doubted if either Colonel Johnston or Black Dillon would have any idea why Red Campbell had done what he had. They would probably consider him a fool for risking his life to save men who worked for his enemy.

"I reckon Morse and Campbell didn't shake hands after they got above ground again," Ives said dryly.

"Not exactly," Randy grinned. "But each has a lot of respect for the other."

Ives broke off the talk and returned to his roulette table.

Randy swung to the saddle and rode to the Elephant Corral. Cotting was asleep on a bunk in his office. His face, wrinkled as a winter pippin left too long, looked old and tired. The young man did not awaken him. He must have been busy for hours slipping to and fro nailing posters to walls and doors while nobody was looking. Two of them were attached to the adobe wall of the corral. Randy watered and fed his horse, then went to the rooming house where he had stayed before he moved to Three Cedars.

It was close to noon when he awakened. After breakfasting he walked down to the Elephant Corral. Cotting had been expecting him for hours. Having found Randy's horse in a stall, he knew its owner had returned.

"I tacked up more than fifty of your posters," he said, his eyes bright with excitement. "Believe me, I had to do a lot of sneakin' around not to get caught but I sure did a job. Seeing I didn't want Johnston to get sore about being left out, I put two on his house, one on the bank, and another right spang on the wall of the Wagon Wheel."

"You did a great job, Limpy. I'm sure

202

obliged. Hope you burned the copies you did not use. I'd hate for the colonel to find them here."

"He won't. I done got rid of them." The old man chuckled. "Jim Tolt, the swamper at the Wagon Wheel, told me old False Face went into a dither when he found out about the placards. Since half the folks in town hate his guts he don't know who to blame."

"Keep it under your hat, Limpy. He'll do his best to find out who stuck them up."

Cotting had a lot of questions to ask about the trouble at the mines. MacNeill told him briefly. It was time he reported to his employer. He knew that Johnston must have heard of his arrival and would be angry at the delay in seeing him.

A cowboy sitting in a game of stud at the Wagon Wheel intercepted him to ask questions about the fight between Morse and Campbell. At this time of day the gaming house had few customers. Ives strolled over to the poker table to listen.

Black Dillon came out of the office at the far corner of the hall. He said curtly, "The colonel wants to see you in the office right damn now."

"Headed that way," Randy answered.

He stopped to answer another question put by Ives. When he reached the office a couple of minutes later Johnston was fuming at the delay. During the past few days everything had gone wrong for him. Now this insolent young pup had kept him waiting for hours.

"When did you reach town?" Johnston snapped.

"About two o'clock in the night. I came here but you were gone. Ives said you had got the wind up over some doggerel that had been nailed up around town and headed for home with Dillon."

Johnston's face turned red. "Never mind about that. Where have you been all morning? It's nearly one now."

"I overslept, Colonel," Randy said innocently. "Then I had a bit of breakfast, fed my horse, and came to tell what I know."

"When you do a job for me come straight to me with a report. Understand? Don't stop to gab with every Tom, Dick, and Harry."

"I didn't know Mr. Ives came in that list," Randy apologized.

"Don't twist my meaning," Johnston flung back angrily. He was in a vile temper, both enraged and frightened, in a mood to rip loose against anyone whom it was safe to attack. Metzger had already felt the lash of his tongue. "You know I don't mean Ives. I've been waiting for you for hours."

"Sorry, Colonel. Didn't know I was so important." Randy looked down at his soiled and ragged trousers. "I hate to show up like this, but I didn't stop at your store to buy me a new pair of pants before I came."

"What the hell does it matter how *you* look?" Black Dillon cut in contemptuously.

"Let's have it," Johnston said, patience worn thin. "What did you find out about the plans of those two scoundrels to murder me? I hear you were thick as three in a bed with them."

"Thought that was why I was sent there," Randy answered with soft irony. "Morse and Metzger wanted to know why for, but I kept my mouth clamped as ordered. I found out this. Campbell and Scanlan will fight to a finish to keep the Argonaut, but they have no notion of starting any trouble. Fact is they are not dead sure MacNeill wasn't shot in a drunken row."

"That's exactly what happened," Dillon agreed quickly.

"The guy is washed out and buried," Randy said with callous indifference. "Does it matter who bumped him?"

"It does if MacNeill's ghost is haunting certain people," Dillon said with his usual insolence.

Johnston ignored his guard. "It doesn't matter if you are sure about the Argonaut claim jumpers." Johnston picked up one of the posters and pushed it across the table to MacNeill. "But it does matter that last night this town was plastered with this threat against me. I want to know who did it."

Randy read it, a puzzled frown on his face. "I don't get what this silly stuff about Jesse James means," he said.

"So it is silly, you think. I don't. It means that I'm to be murdered as Bob Ford was after killing Jesse James." He added in explanation, "The inference is that I had Tom MacNeill killed."

"Did you?" Randy asked with cool effrontery.

"Cut out the impudence, Burns. I won't take it. Of course I didn't."

"Looks to me you are safe enough even if you did hire the fellow drygulched. You have Mr. Dillon's tried and true gun beside you every minute."

"Keep your tongue off my name, Burns," the Shadow ordered, hatred lying deep in his opaque eyes. "For a two-spot in the deck you are too biggity."

MacNeill's cold hard eyes measured the guard for a long moment. He felt that the man was as deadly as a cobra. "Lookin' at it one way a two-spot is next to the ace," he said.

Johnston rapped on the table with his

knuckles. "I'll do the talking," he snapped. "Metzger brings a bad report from the mines. He says Morse has gone soft and wants to baby the Argonaut ore thieves. Know anything about that, Burns?"

"Yes, I know something about it," Randy replied. "Morse is a tough hard-rock miner, about as soft as a blacksmith's hammer. He'd take on John L. Sullivan quick as a wink. But he is not a gun fighter. And his feeling toward the Argonaut men sure has changed. That's true of all your men in Three Cedars. Campbell is a sort of hero to them. If anything happened to him or his partner there would be a terrible rookus, and I'm afraid the blame would be laid to you." He leaned forward, his eyes on Johnston, and added, his voice packed in ice, "Say the word and I'll knock them off and light out."

"And leave me holding the sack," Johnston said bitterly.

"Give this upstart the job and he'll muff it certain," Dillon jeered. "It don't pay to send a boy to mill, Colonel."

Johnston ignored his guard's annoyance. "You think Morse would not back any play I made," he said to MacNeill.

"The whole camp has got it in mind to protect them if necessary," Randy replied bluntly.

"An accident might happen," Johnston suggested.

"Not at the mine. Morse would be on it like a terrier on a rat. He wouldn't stand for it."

"I'll have to sack Morse soon as I can get someone to take his place," Johnston said thoughtfully. "I won't have disloyal men working for me."

"Why all the fuss?" Dillon wanted to know impatiently. "Just say the word and I'll handle these two fellows. To hell with Morse. I'm getting tired of all this shilly-shallying around."

Johnston did not say the word. Randy guessed that he was much disturbed. He was afraid of stirring up dormant hate to rise and engulf him. He had spent years putting his empire together and now he could feel it breaking away under him.

"We'll wait for a time," he said. "Meanwhile you have another job, Burns. Find out who is pulling off this wall-placarding business. Let me see if you are worth your salt."

"Got any idea about who is back of it?" Randy asked.

"Somebody who hates me and wants me dead. That's all I know."

"That cuts it down to not more than three fifths of the people in the county," Dillon jeered. "Post a big reward and there will be a sure enough massacre of innocents."

"This is no time for buffoonery, Black," his employer reproved. To Randy he said, "Go at this discreetly without letting anybody know it is important. I expect results."

He waved a hand toward the door in dismissal of Randy.

Chapter Twenty-five

Randy walked out of the office pleased with himself. By playing on Johnston's timidity he had won postponement of any action against his friends. Not that postponement was a victory. It only relieved the pressure on Scanlan and Campbell, but the time gained might be used to advantage. He didn't know how, exactly, although he had a vague idea that if he had enough time, he could keep the pressure on Johnston by using the Jesse James song. It was possible to break the man. He was convinced of that. Then his whole empire would crumble.

Randy's satisfaction lasted for one short moment only. A solidly built fellow wearing a derby hat was pushing through the batwing half doors into the gambling hall. The man was Clift Walker. The time Randy had gained in one place had been lost in another.

There was nobody Randy wanted to meet less than Walker. The gambler must know from common gossip that he had stayed for weeks at White Rocks looking after Tom when he was wounded. He probably knew that they had come to that town together after the rescue of Tom and that they had put up their horses at the same corral. He had tipped Black Dillon as to the best spot for an ambush. It was possible he knew who had fired the bullet that tore into the killer's arm. One whispered sentence to Dillon might be enough to destroy Randy.

Walker moved forward to the roulette table and introduced himself to Ives. As he talked his slitted eyes slid restlessly about the room. It struck Randy he was uncertain of his welcome here. Perhaps he felt it was not safe to know as much as he did.

Randy sauntered to the roulette table and greeted the tinhorn cheerfully. "If it ain't Clift Walker," he exclaimed. "When did you hit this burg, old-timer?"

The gambler looked at him with startled eyes. What was this Burns doing here? And why the glad hand? At White Rocks Burns had shown no friendliness toward him.

"Ten minutes ago," he said guardedly. "I'm just sorta driftin' around, you might say."

"Fine. Bet you are as hungry as a winter wolf." Randy slipped his arm under Walker's elbow. "We'll mosey down to Win Sing's restaurant and have us a feed while we have a powwow over old times."

Walker did not understand this and was reluctant to accept the invitation. "I figured I would have a drink or two before I ate," he evaded.

"Sure. Right here at the bar."

Watching the men, Ives felt there was something false about this situation. "You two old friends?" he asked.

"Used to board at the same place," Randy explained cheerfully. "Let's go get that drink, Clift."

The tinhorn found himself being propelled gently but firmly toward the bar. His host kept a stream of talking going to drown his protests. Glumly he drank and with MacNeill still glued to his arm presently reached the sidewalk on his way to the restaurant.

Walker jerked himself free. "Lay off me, fellow. I don't like a hair of your head and you got no use for me."

"Right," Randy agreed. "If I had my way, I'd take your hair off your head about scalp-deep, but I don't want a killing here. Haven't you got sense enough to stay away from Tail Holt?"

"Why?"

"You know too much."

"I don't get what you mean," Walker said sullenly.

"Oh, yes you do. You spotted Tom Mac-Neill for Black Dillon — told him where to wait so he could get the drop on MacNeill. Haven't you got an ounce of brains? You are the only man who can tie Black up with the killing. So like a chump you come here and remind him of it. Either get out or go order your coffin."

Walker stared at him from worried eyes. "Black wouldn't do that to me," he protested.

"Wouldn't he?" Randy grinned. There was a grimness about the grin that did not comfort the tinhorn. "You've got a different opinion of him than I have. Maybe you are right. Maybe every time he sees you he won't think, *Here's a guy that can send me to the gallows.* Maybe he has got religion and turned soft."

"I don't know a thing against Black," Walker bleated. "You've got me all wrong."

"Good. After all if I'm right it will be your funeral."

They sat at a table for two. Win Sing served the dinner and Randy did not press the matter of the other man's departure. He was of the

212

opinion that after he had eaten Walker would saddle up and leave.

Meanwhile the gambler's thoughts had shifted to another angle of the situation. Burns had been a friend of the murdered Tom MacNeill. What was he doing in Johnston's town?

He voiced the question bluntly. Randy explained that he was one of the colonel's gunmen and that he had been in White Rocks on business of his boss. "A protection man doesn't have friends," he said.

They were pushing back their chairs to rise when Black Dillon walked into the room. He stopped, eyes narrowed with suspicion, to stare at these two. What he saw he did not like. Why had Walker come to town? And for what reason was he eating with Burns?

He ignored Randy. To Walker he said, "I want to talk with you, fellow."

Walker looked as if he had been shot at and barely missed. He said shakily, "It's — it's nice to meet you again, Mr. Dillon."

The Shadow turned his back on him and walked out of the restaurant. Walker followed him unhappily. He suggested to Randy a schoolboy on his way to the principal's office for a severe thrashing.

Young MacNeill wasted no sympathy on the tinhorn. He had himself to think about. A rug had been pulled out from under him. Inside of ten minutes Dillon would know a good deal about him, and from what he learned from Walker he'd be able to guess more. Randy had to get out in a hurry unless he wanted to shoot it out with the bunch of them. He didn't. Johnston was the man he wanted.

Randy paid the pigtailed Win Sing four bits for two dinners. Before he left the restaurant he made sure his six-shooter lay lightly in its holster. There was a chance that within the next few minutes a fraction of a second in the draw might make the difference between life and death for him.

He did not want it that way. Dillon was too expert a gunman, too deadly a killer, for a young cowboy to face with any likelihood of coming out alive. Randy counted himself a good shot, one of the best he had known on the range, and more than once he had played with the thought that someday he might meet the Shadow with a blazing gun in his hand, but now that such a meeting seemed imminent a cold weight chilled his stomach. He shrank from the dreadful risk.

Randy walked into the sunlit street after first making sure his enemy was not standing in wait for him. Dillon and Walker were just disappearing in the doorway of the Wagon

Wheel. It was the siesta hour and the only other persons on the street were Ingrid Carlson and her cousin Polly Edgar. They were approaching Win Sing's place not thirty yards away. Two lovely innocents with no place in this hell hole of hate.

Polly cried, "It's that strange man who doesn't come to see us any more. He doesn't like us."

Randy looked at Ingrid, wondering if she remembered why he had not called on the Edgars when he had been in town before going to Three Cedars. He brought his gaze to Polly's eager young face. "Now you know that isn't true," Randy denied. "I just reached town and can't come calling in these awful clothes — not on Miss Polly Edgar and her family."

"That's just an excuse," Polly flung back. "Not long ago you promised Father to come that night and didn't."

The grave eyes of Ingrid met those of Randy. "We just passed somebody who was talking about you. I caught a few words. He doesn't like you." There was a look in those anxious eyes he had never seen before.

Randy mentioned the name of the man. "Black Dillon."

"What have you done to make him angry?" Ingrid asked.

"The man walking with him has just told him I am a friend of Tom MacNeill."

"Who is the man with him?"

"Clift Walker. He is the man who put the finger on Tom for Dillon to kill."

The color died out of Polly's cheeks and lips. "You don't mean — you can't mean that . . ." The sentence froze in her throat. "Oh, hurry — hurry and get away."

"Polly is right. You can't stay here." Ingrid spoke urgently. "Why aren't you saddling your horse?"

"We seem to be all of one mind," Randy said cheerfully, of no intent to let them know how disturbed he was. "If I run away I may live to fight another day."

Ingrid did not tell him that she had warned him it would turn out this way. She said, "You'll be trapped for sure — unless you are out of town before they close in on you."

"It might be Walker doesn't know as much as I think he does. There is a chance I could stay and bluff it out." He added, to cut off Ingrid's sharp impatient retort, "But not a good enough one. I'll light a shuck. You girls had better go home, just in case. *Vaya con Dios.*"

Both girls watched him as he went down the street, a slender brown man dressed like a tramp but one whose rippling muscles carried him with a lithe and easy grace. He was so young, so reckless, and so likable, and in a few minutes that strong body might be lying lifeless in the dirt. So lean and gay, so iron-hard, so boyish, yet probably doomed to death before the sun set.

Polly turned to her cousin for reassurance. "Do you think — he will be all right?" she asked unhappily.

"Yes," Ingrid told her firmly. "He'll be out of town in five minutes." But they were only words. A chill wind of fear was blowing through her. Only now when she realized how much danger he was in did the truth come to her. She was in love with him.

Randy walked rapidly to his boarding-house, paid the bill, and packed his belongings in a blanket roll. It was not far to the Elephant Corral, but every foot of the way his shifting eyes swept the street. He did not know how much time he had, but if this business worked the way he thought it would, he had only a few minutes, perhaps less.

With the Shadow's help Johnston must be at this moment dragging out of Walker all he knew or suspected. Very likely they might think there was no hurry, that Randy was not alerted to the danger. Knowing the men, he guessed that Black Dillon would be crowding his boss for instant action and that the colonel as usual would want to play it safe. A shot in the dark from an unknown killer would leave no evidence to implicate anybody. If that was the decision the roads out of town would be watched to make sure he did not leave. But Dillon, stabbing at a guess that it was Randy who had wounded him at White Rocks, would probably override Johnston for a quick kill.

"They are on to me," Randy barked at Cotting. "I'm on the run."

His horse was in the pasture back of the corral. He took the rope from the saddle, walked into the pasture, and dropped the loop over the animal's head.

At the corral he set the saddle blanket in place, swung the saddle across the back of the horse, and reached for the cinch.

Cotting was standing on the other side of the shack. Now his high-pitched voice, quavering with excitement, brought Randy to sharp attention.

"Visitors headin' this way to see us," it announced.

Chapter Twenty-six

As Black Dillon with his captive companion passed through the big gaming room of the Wagon Wheel to the office Ives observed them with a living curiosity. First Burns and now the Shadow had the fellow Clift Walker in tow and on both occasions he looked dejected and unhappy. The croupier decided that in a few minutes he would join them and find out what the mysterious link was that tied them together.

Dillon opened the door and pushed his companion into the office. They interrupted a talk between Johnston and Metzger about the profits of the house for the past week. The colonel's guard crashed into it abruptly.

"Maybe you would like to know that you are paying this fellow Burns to spy on us," Dillon snarled. "And that is not all. He was a friend of Tom MacNeill and nursed him till he died."

Johnston's bland face showed shock. "I don't believe it."

"You just don't want to admit you made a mistake, but you did. It would have been a hell of a lot bigger one if I hadn't found out the truth."

"Have you evidence to prove what you're saying?" Johnston asked.

"Tell your story, Walker," Dillon ordered.

He told it, prompted by Dillon a dozen times. According to Walker, MacNeill and this Burns had reached White Rocks together the day after MacNeill had been released from captivity by the killing of Sowder. They came together to the Trail End Hotel but after the first night pretended that they did not know each other. Burns was the first man on the spot after MacNeill was shot down. He had a pistol in his hand.

Dillon interrupted. "He was the fellow that shot me. I'm dead sure of it now. I wish I had known it an hour or two ago."

"He was the one all right," Walker agreed, and went on to say that Burns had stayed at the hotel until MacNeill died and then had taken his body away for burial.

Ives had come into the room and was listening. "I thought it was queer the way Burns latched on to Walker and steered him out of the Wagon Wheel." On his lips was a thin, satiric smile. "You have to admit the kid is good, Colonel. He worked you to a fare-you-well."

Dillon slammed his fist on the table. "Hell's hinges, he must have been one of the crowd that killed Sowder."

Ives drawled softly, "If so, he sure earned a star for that."

"We must do something about this," Johnston said worriedly. "Right away. He must not under any circumstances talk to the sheriff. He knows enough to send all you boys to prison."

"And you too, Colonel," Dillon added. "Don't forget that."

"You can leave me out of it," Ives mentioned. "He hasn't got a thing on me. Nobody has."

Johnston's handsome face showed strain. "We must take action — tonight."

"Say what you mean, Colonel. Blast him to hell." Dillon's voice was implacably cruel. "But we won't wait until tonight. We'll do it now."

"We must use judgment, Black," his employer differed. "Handle him the way you did MacNeill. A shot in the dark, and nobody will know who fired it."

"He might get the wind up and hit the road if we wait," Metzger objected. "Then we would have our neck in a noose."

"We could guard the roads," Johnston said, "and see that he doesn't leave town. We don't want any backfire over this."

"I'm going to kill him right in the open within ten minutes," Dillon announced, his face a frozen mask of hate. "You can cut out the talk. You're just wasting time. I'm taking charge of this."

"Why don't you gang up on him?" Ives jeered. "That would be safer."

Dillon glared at the gambler, "I'm not looking for help. I'll do the job myself." He turned to Metzger. "Dolph, you and Walker go down to the Elephant Corral and drive away any horses that are in the corral or the pasture. I don't want him to skip out before I get to him. If he has any sense he'll be plenty worried right now."

"I don't think your way of handling this is the best, Black," Johnston said. "But if you have made up your mind there is no stopping you."

"That's right," Dillon said. "Nothing will stop me."

"Do you aim to give the kid a chance for his white alley?" Calhoun Ives asked coolly. "If not, this town will raise hell. It would not take much to set it off, either. That may be something you don't know, Colonel."

Johnston turned on the croupier angrily. "I don't understand your attitude, Ives. I don't like it. Are you for us or against us? Do you

222

think we ought to sit with hands folded and let this spy ruin our whole setup?"

Ives, his eyes icy cold, looked at his employer with an insolence that bordered on contempt. The gambler had always treated him with reasonable courtesy before. Of all the men who worked for Johnston, only Black Dillon had been openly insolent. But now there could be no doubt about the way Calhoun Ives felt toward his boss.

"I'm your hired gun, Colonel," Ives said. "At least I have been, but I am my own man. Do what you want to with this kid. I'm not interfering, but I don't have to like it. And another thing. I tell you I know the temper of the town. You are building up trouble for yourself."

"So you are worried about me," Johnston said with irritable displeasure.

"Not enough to keep me awake nights," Ives drawled. "Fact is, since you are asking for it, I kinda admire the kid. He has brains and guts and a you-be-damned way about him. If you have him pegged right you know he is the kind who stands by his friends to the end. Say I was in a jam and he was for me I'd pick him mighty quick for a side kick."

"You'll never get a chance," Dillon retorted. "He has come to the last mile of his crooked trail."

Ives laughed. "Did you say crooked?"

Dillon ignored the question. He motioned to Metzger and Walker. "Get going, Dolph. Make sure there isn't a horse left for him at the corral. I'm headin' for his rooming place first. He may be packing to fog out."

He walked out of the room, at the heels of Metzger and Walker. Ives would have followed if Johnston hadn't said, "Wait."

Ives stood in the doorway looking at the banker. He said, "Well?"

"I want to know where you stand," Johnston said. "I've paid you well. I have a right to know whether I still have your loyalty."

"Colonel," Ives said, "I think you know how I stand. There are certain things I will do as long as you are paying for my gun. If the Halloran gang attacked Tail Holt, or if they came back to the Wagon Wheel to raise hell like they did the other night, my gun would go to work. But I am not Black Dillon who went to White Rocks and gunned MacNeill down without giving him a chance. And I want no part of hunting young Burns down and giving him what MacNeill got."

"We are all in this together," Johnston cried. "Burns can ruin everything, but you tell me you want no part of — of — " He could not make himself finish the sentence.

Ives smiled. He understood Johnston.

Long ago he had seen behind the mask of piety that the banker habitually wore. He said, "Kinda hard to put your tongue to a word like murder, isn't it, Colonel? That is what it was with MacNeill. It will be the same with Burns if Dillon gets a chance. Sooner or later, Colonel, your whole empire will fall on your head. It always happens when you build a fortune on murder and that is exactly what you have done."

"I will not stand for your insolence," Johnston stormed. "You're fired. Get out of town."

"Thank you, Colonel," Ives said. "I'll get out of the Wagon Wheel, but I may not leave town. I told you a minute ago I wouldn't interfere. Maybe I will, now that I'm fired."

"I didn't mean what I said." Johnston saw he had made a mistake. "Stay until this business is finished. I will double your pay. We don't know what will happen now. Burns may get out of town and ride to High Grass Valley. He might throw in with the Halloran gang and bring them to Tail Holt."

"No, I'm fired," Ives said. "It was the best news I've had for a long time. I have had a stomachful of you and Dillon and Metzger and your whole bunch." The gambler started to go out of the room and then turned back. "Colonel, I don't think Burns will go after the Hallorans. He is here because he knows you are responsible for Tom MacNeill's death and I don't think he will leave town until he has evened the score. Good day, Colonel." Ives nodded and left the room.

Chapter Twenty-Seven

For a moment Randy remained motionless when he heard Cotting say visitors were headed their way. If he made a stand here, Limpy might be pulled into the fight and he didn't want that to happen. But if he decided to run for it with Johnston's wolf pack on his tail, he would be nailed sooner or later.

He tightened the cinch, calling, "How many, Limpy?"

"Two of 'em. Metzger and that tinhorn Walker."

Randy was both relieved and puzzled. If they knew he was here and had come for him, Dillon would be with them. So they must have come for some other purpose. But what?

"Don't let on I'm here," Randy said. "Find out what they're up to."

Metzger and Walker were approaching from the direction of the Wagon Wheel.

Randy was on the opposite side of Cotting's shack, so he hadn't been seen. That gave him an advantage that he aimed to play for all it was worth. It suited him if it came to gun play. He was certain Walker would not fight. That would make it even, Randy against Dolph Metzger. He could not expect any better odds than that.

He waited for what seemed several minutes, then he heard Cotting yell, "What do you think you're doing, Metzger?" There was no answer. A moment later Cotting shouted furiously, "Get away from that gate, Metzger. Walker, get out of my pasture. I ain't letting you run them horses into the road."

"Stay where you are, old man," Metzger said. "We don't aim to let you get into trouble by allowing this fellow Burns to steal one of your horses and get out of town."

It was time for Randy to take a hand. Feeling the way he did toward Johnston, Limpy was bound to get himself into real trouble with Metzger. Randy stepped around the corner of the shack, calling, "You won't do any good running those horses into the road, Metzger. I've already got mine."

Walker was in the pasture. Metzger stood at the gate. He was startled and unnerved by Randy's sudden appearance. Behind him Walker lifted his hands and screamed, "I'm not in this, Burns. They made me come."

Metzger licked his lips, his face pale. He was remembering how this young devil had handled his gun the night Butch Halloran's gang was in town. That was the only time he had ever actually seen Burns use a gun, but he had heard him talk, and he knew how Burns had performed in Three Cedars.

He stared at Burns standing at the corner of Cotting's shack, a lithe stringy man balanced just a little forward, his right hand at his side. Metzger could turn around and run. But he was not sure that Burns wouldn't shoot him in the back. Besides, if he did run and got away, he would never live it down. Johnston paid him well, but it was for his gun, not because he had a great talent for managing the Wagon Wheel. Then he thought, *Burns is just a kid, a Johnny-come-lately. If I get him, I'll be ahead of Dillon.*

Randy watched Metzger's face. He saw the indecision, the conflict between this desire to run and his pride that held him there. Randy had pegged the man before. He was soft, lacking the callous hardness that was in Black Dillon and the tough integrity of the gambler, Calhoun Ives. But soft or not, Metzger had his tail in a crack. He had hired out to Johnston as a hardcase and had taken his money. Now there was no backing out. He made his play as Randy had been sure he would. There was nothing else he could do.

Metzger's hand slashed downward for his gun. Randy let him have the advantage of making the first move, but it was not enough for Dolph Metzger. His gun was never fired. Randy's bullet caught him in the chest and knocked him back against the adobe wall of the corral. His heels dug a furrow in the dust as his feet slid forward, then he fell sideways.

Randy said, his gun on Metzger, "Take a look at him, Limpy."

Cotting let out a whoop. "You got him, boy. I don't need to look."

Randy motioned to Walker. "Come here."

The gambler walked out of the pasture, sweat breaking through the skin of his face. He looked at Metzger's motionless body, shuddered and turned his head, and came to where Randy stood, hands still above his shoulders. "You wouldn't kill me, Burns. I'm not going to make a try for my gun."

"Why shouldn't I kill you?" Randy asked. "You put the finger on Tom MacNeill in White Rocks. Dillon was the one who shot him, wasn't he?"

"Yeah, it was Dillon." Walker stared at the ground. "I had to put the finger on MacNeill. Dillon made me."

Randy looked at Cotting. "Is there a law

against killing a liar, Limpy?"

"Not in my book," Cotting said happily. "All liars should be shot between the eyes."

Randy nodded. "Right between the eyes."

Walker began backing up. "You — you couldn't do that."

"I could," Randy said, "but I won't if you go to Johnston and tell him what happened to Metzger. Tell him that Scanlan was talking about going after the Halloran gang. Ask him what he thinks will happen to him when Campbell and Scanlan and me and the Halloran bunch all show up in Tail Holt at one time. Tell him I'm leaving town but I won't be riding far. I'll be back."

Walker was trembling and sweat was running down his face. "I'll tell him," he whispered.

"Have him send somebody to get Metzger's body," Randy said. "Then get out of town. I won't be soft on you again. If I ever see — "

"You won't see me in Tail Holt again," Walker said. "Not ever again."

"All right, go see Johnston," Randy ordered.

Walker turned and started to run. Cotting said, "He can run faster. Put a bullet into the dust at his feet."

"It would be a waste of lead." Randy holstered his gun and mounted. "Keep your eyes

230

open, Limpy. Dillon may pay you a visit to find out where I went."

"Don't tell me where you're headed," Cotting said. "If I don't know, I can't tell him."

"Maybe you had better come with me."

The old man's mouth set stubbornly. "I'm staying. I have a business to run and I aim to run it." His lips relaxed into a grin. "I sure admire the way you handle your iron, boy. It wasn't no fluke that night when you shot the gun out of Tiny Shep Steelman's hand." A question occurred to him. "Say, are you going to High Grass Valley to join up with Halloran?"

Randy shook his head. "I could use some help, but there isn't time. I wouldn't do it anyway. That would be like inviting another wolf pack to fight Johnston's wolves. Between them all the sheep in town would be killed."

"I guess that's right," Cotting agreed, "but you can't play a lone hand."

"I figure I can," Randy said. "There's one less wolf in the pack now. If Dillon shows up, just tell him I'll be back. I'll either shoot Johnston or scare him to death. So long, Limpy."

Randy rode out of town as if he were headed for High Grass Valley. He considered going to Three Cedars and getting Scanlan and Campbell, then dismissed the thought. It would take too long. He knew what the death

231

of Metzger would do to a man as timid as Johnston. As long as the czar had the power he possessed now, not only in Tail Holt but in Three Cedars and White Rocks too, there would be no safety for Scanlan or Campbell. Tom could not return. Now that Randy was exposed to Johnston, he was in the same boat.

Johnston would retain his power as long as he was alive. Killing Metzger had accomplished nothing because another man would be hired to take his place. Or a dozen of them if Johnston decided he needed that many.

It was the same with Dillon, but when Randy thought about facing the guard, some of the confidence left him. Dillon and Metzger were men of different caliber. And what about Calhoun Ives? He had no respect for Johnston. Dillon did not, either, but the high wages he received would be enough of an attraction to hold him. It might not work that way with Ives. Randy wished he could talk with the gambler, but that was impossible.

When Randy was hidden among the hills, he began to circle, riding warily and stopping often to listen. He did not know whether there would be a pursuit or not, but if there was, he hoped he would not be placed in a position where he would have to make a run for it. He wanted to be back in town shortly after it was dark.

By midafternoon he was convinced Johnston had decided to let him return to town rather than chase him. He reached Tail Holt Creek and followed it downstream, not stopping until he reached the spot where he had first met Ingrid Carlson.

He dismounted, loosened the cinch, and sat down to wait for darkness. His thoughts turned to the handsome, slender girl he had seen for the first time at this very place. He had loved her from that moment, although he had not been aware of it at the time. Now he wondered if he would ever see her again, and would she understand why he was doing what he had to do?

Chapter Twenty-eight

Black Dillon's hatred for the young man he knew as Lloyd Burns was a consuming fire in him. He had been jealous of Burns from the first. He had foreseen the possibility of the fellow taking his place in Colonel Johnston's organization. Burns had all the qualifications, he was younger, and he would probably work for less money. It was not a question of Dillon having any affection for his employer. He did not even honestly respect Johnston, but his position with the banker gave him a great deal of prestige in Tail Holt. He did not want to lose it.

When Dillon left the office in the Wagon Wheel, he went directly to Burns's rooming house, intent on killing him at sight. The fact that Walker had confirmed his suspicions about the young devil added fuel to the flame of his fury. Burns had been a spy. He undoubtedly knew that Dillon was Tom MacNeill's murderer. And, to top it all, Burns must have been the one who had wounded Dillon.

So, with his right hand on gun butt, Dillon used his left to knock on the door of the rooming house. If Burns had opened the door, Dillon would have pulled his gun and shot him without hesitation. But it was the landlady, Mrs. Cramer, who opened the door, a gentle, white-haired woman who recoiled in terror when she looked at Dillon's hard brown face upon which was marked so clearly the promise of death.

"I want to see Burns," Dillon said.

"He's gone," Mrs. Cramer told him. "He paid me for his room and packed up and left just a little while ago."

"Don't lie to me," Dillon said. "Which room does he have?"

"He had the northeast corner room, but I told you he left — "

Dillon pushed her aside and ran up the stairs. He shoved the door of Burns's room open, his gun in his hand. Mrs. Cramer had not lied. The fellow had moved out just as she had said. Dillon raced back down the stairs, shouting at Mrs. Cramer, "Where did he go?"

"I don't know," she cried. "You do not have any authority to come — "

He grabbed her by the arm and shook her. "Where is he?"

"I told you I don't know. He just took his things and left. I suppose he went to the Elephant Corral where he kept his horse — "

Dillon whirled and ran out of the house. He should have known that was what Burns would do. The young devil was no fool. He was fogging out of town just as Dillon had guessed he would, but he had moved faster than Dillon had thought possible. Johnston was an old maid and wanted to play everything safe. If Dillon waited for his employer to make a move —

Gun shots exploded from the direction of the Elephant Corral. Dillon slowed up. Metzger and Walker must have caught Burns before he got away.

The Elephant Corral was in the other end of town from Mrs. Cramer's rooming house.

235

When Dillon got there, young Burns was gone and Dolph Metzger was dead, his body still on the ground beside the adobe wall of the corral. Walker was nowhere in sight but old Limpy Cotting was in the shack he used for an office.

"Cotting," Dillon yelled.

The guard could not believe this had happened. He had always considered Metzger more blow than anything else, a man with a good front but weak on guts when the showdown came. But he still should have been faster with a gun than a working cowboy like Lloyd Burns just off the range.

Cotting came out of the shack. "I guess Walker will have somebody come and get the body. If you want to take it — "

"No, I don't want to take it," Dillon snarled. "Just tell me what happened."

Cotting told him. Then he said, "Walker sure didn't want to die. He got his hands up pronto and started yelling his head off that he wasn't in the rookus."

"Where did Burns go?"

"I don't know," Cotting said. "He told Walker he was leaving town but he would not be riding far."

"Quit lying," Dillon roared. "Where is he?"

"I told you I didn't know," the old man

236

said. "I can't tell you something I don't know."

Dillon hit him on one side of the head with an open palm, a savage blow that rocked his head, and then struck him on the other cheek. "Answer my question, Cotting, or by God you will wish you had. Was Burns going after the Hallorans or was he aiming to get Johnston?"

Cotting stumbled back and leaned against the wall of the shack. He looked at the gunman, hating him. "I don't know nothing about the Hallorans. All I know is that he will get Johnston and he will get you. Hit me again, Dillon. That is your size, but I won't tell you no more because I don't know no more."

Dillon stared at the old man. He wanted to kill him. He was Burns's friend. He had more sand in his craw than most of the Tail Holt men. When Burns came back, he might side the young cowboy. But it would not do to kill Cotting right out here in the open in broad daylight. He turned on his heel and walked down the street toward the Wagon Wheel.

Walker was in the office with Johnston. Dillon closed the door and stood with his back to it. He said, "Burns got out of town." Johnston did not say anything. His face was as white as his hair. One corner of his mouth was jerking with the same rhythm that his pulse was beating in his forehead. Dillon's lips curled in disgust.

"What are you scared of, Colonel?" Dillon asked.

Johnston fumbled in his coat pocket for a cigar. He said, "Walker tells me Burns is bringing Scanlan and Campbell to town. He is going after the Hallorans, too." He licked his lips. "Metzger is dead. Ives quit. We can't match their strength, Black."

"Ives quit?"

"Well, I fired him and then I said I did not mean it and I would double his wages, but he said that firing him was the best news he had heard for a long time."

"So you fired him. You picked a good time, Colonel." He motioned to Walker. "Get out of here. I ought to kill you. You could have drilled Burns while he was smoking Metzger down, but you were yellow."

Walker scurried out through the door. Dillon shut it and walked to the desk. "Your luck has run out, Colonel. They are closing in on you. Ives warned you. He said he knew the temper of the town. He was right. You know what happens when the lead wolf goes down. The rest of them jump on him, too."

Dillon turned toward the door. Johnston cried, "What are you going to do, Black?"

Dillon put a hand on the knob of the office door and looked back. "It is time to go,

Colonel." He waited. He had his employer exactly where he wanted him.

"You can't do that. You have been with me a long time. We — "

Johnston stopped. Dillon said, "Sure, we have been together a long time, and we've been through a lot, with me saving your hide more times than I can count. Now you want me to save your hide again. Well, I warned you about Burns, but you would not listen. You had to have a man to take Sowder's place." The insolent smile was on Dillon's lips. "You are a smart man in some ways, Colonel, but in other ways you are a complete fool, and a coward to boot.

Johnston did not reprimand him this time for his insolence. He asked, "What do you want, Black?"

"That's better." Dillon dropped his hand from the knob. "Start thinking about what will happen to you if I pull out. If I stay, I will write my own ticket. I have taken a lot of chances with my life to pull you out of the holes you fall into. From now on you will pay me something worthwhile or you will stay in the hole you are in."

"What is your ticket?"

"A free hand with our men," Dillon said. "I run everything my way without having you drag your heels or having somebody like

Metzger or Ives giving orders."

"You are too rash to take charge," Johnston said weakly. "We must use caution — "

"A cautious man will hang sooner than a rash one," Dillon broke in. "And one more thing. I am your partner if I stay. Fifty-fifty!"

Johnston slumped in his chair. Beads of sweat on his face glistened in the afternoon sunlight that fell through the west window. He stood up, gripping the edge of the desk. "Black, I cannot do that. You are a gun guard and a good one, but you are not a businessman. I have paid you well — "

"Take it or leave it, Colonel," Dillon reached for the doorknob again. "It sounds like you are leaving it. You will see you made a mistake about the time Butch Halloran and Tiny Shep Steelman and the rest of that bunch of toughs hit town."

Johnston dropped back into his chair. "All right," he said heavily. "I will draw up the proper papers. While I am doing that, I suggest you put our men on the roads so we will be warned in time. If Burns comes back by himself, we will know it."

"I intended to do that," Dillon said, and left the office.

Ives was not around. Dillon gave the orders and none of the men objected. Apparently they recognized his leadership now that Metzger

240

and Ives were both gone. After the men left, Dillon had a drink at the bar. He wondered if Johnston was capable of killing a man. He did not think so, but sometimes a coward will do strange things if he is pushed enough. Perhaps Dillon had forced too hard a bargain upon Johnston.

Well, he could discuss that with his new partner later. Right now he had to take care of young Burns. He was sure Cotting had told the truth when he had said he did not know whether Burns had gone after the Hallorans or not. It seemed to Dillon, Burns being the kind he was, that he would come back after dark and make a try for Johnston. If he was calling it right, all he had to do was to stay close to Johnston.

Dillon took another drink, a new idea occurring to him. Burns might not have left town. But who would have the courage to hide him in Tail Holt? Dillon mentally went over the people in town who might be Burns's friends. Only one family seemed a fair guess. The Edgars!

No other family in town would have the courage to defy Johnston. It did not seem to Dillon that there was much of a chance that Burns would be with the Edgars, but it was enough to warrant visiting them. If they were not hiding him, they might know where he was. His trouble would be in getting the Edgars to tell him where Burns was hiding. He laughed softly as he left the gambling house. Perhaps he could persuade them that Johnston wanted to reward the young man.

Chapter Twenty-nine

When Calhoun Ives walked out of the Wagon Wheel for the last time, he had no intention of leaving Tail Holt immediately. It would be interesting, he thought, to see what happened. He returned to his hotel room and lit a long cigar. He stood by the window looking down into Trail Street, and by the time he had smoked the cigar down to a short stub, it came to him that he had no business staying in Tail Holt at all. He would do well to get out and stay out.

Ives had no stakes in the game either way. His sympathies were with young Burns who would probably circle back and show up in town and get himself killed, but the gambler's sympathies were not enough to make him fight for Burns. His only interest in the cowboy was curiosity as to how he would wind up

242

when he made his play against Colonel Johnston and Black Dillon. That he would make a
play Ives had no doubt. He was that kind of
man.

Ives liked his style, his brashness and
courage, but he was the kind who died young.
That was foolish, the way Ives saw it. He did
not favor any gamble where the odds were
long against him, and Lloyd Burns would be
betting his life against very long odds if he returned to town alone.

Ives was still standing by the window when
he saw Black Dillon leave the Wagon Wheel.
He wondered about it, surprised that Colonel
Johnston would let Dillon out of his sight as
long as Burns was alive. Dillon was known as
the Shadow for good reason.

Impelled by curiosity as much as anything,
Ives left the hotel. He reached the street in
time to see Dillon turn at the end of the block.
When Ives came to the corner, he saw Dillon
go through the gate in front of Doctor Edgar's
house. He hesitated, convinced that the guard
was not making a professional call at the doctor's home. Knowing Dillon as well as he did,
Ives decided he must have some nefarious
purpose of his own.

The gambler hurried his steps. By the time
he reached the gate, Dillon was inside the
house. Ives walked up the path and crossed

the porch to the front door which was still open, alarmed now as he thought about what Dillon was doing. Better than anyone else in Tail Holt he understood the evil purposes and desires which completely dominated the gunman's actions.

From where he stood in the doorway, Ives heard Dillon say, "If you know anything about Burns's whereabouts, you had better tell me. He killed Dolph Metzger today. Colonel Johnston will see to it that he is punished."

"If Lloyd Burns killed a man as you say he did," Ingrid Carlson said hotly, "I am sure it was because he had to."

"I would call it murder," Dillon snapped. "None of us are safe while a murderer is free."

"It would seem to me a matter of the pot calling the kettle black," Ingrid said. "If you want to hold Lloyd Burns for murder, why don't you send for the sheriff? Or have you?"

"No," Dillon answered. "We can handle our own problems in Tail Holt. I see no reason to bother the sheriff. Now answer my question. Do you know where Burns is?"

"No, I do not know."

"Did he go after the Hallorans?"

"I do not know that, either."

"It is my belief that Burns is hidden in this house," Dillon said. "I intend to search it."

"You will not," Ingrid flashed back. "Doctor Edgar was up all night and he is sleeping. I will not permit you to disturb him."

"You won't stop me," Dillon said, and started toward the girl.

Ives stepped through the door, his gun in his hand. "I will if Miss Carlson doesn't," he said.

Dillon whirled, right hand poised over gun butt. He was too surprised to do or say anything for a moment. He stared at the gun in Ives's hand, then at the gambler's hard face. Ives said, "You pull your gun like you are figuring on doing and I will kill you certain. Now get out of the house."

"I thought you were leaving town," Dillon said. "Are you buying chips in this game?"

"Not me." Ives shook his head. "But I don't cotton to the idea of you bullying a woman. Can't you wait for Burns to show up?"

"I guess it would be better if I did," Dillon said.

The guard walked through the door, Ives stepping back and turning so he could watch Dillon until he left the yard.

Ingrid Carlson stood in the doorway. "Thank you, Mr. —— "

"Ives," he supplied. "Of course you do not know me, but I have seen you on the street many times since you came to Tail Holt."

He looked at the girl, admiring her graceful, rounded body, convinced that he would not see her again. He could do no more than admire her, although there had been a day when he had been young and as brash as this cowboy Burns. But that time had been long gone, and now all the Ingrid Carlsons in the world were for men like Burns, not Calhoun Ives.

"I do not know what Dillon would have done," Ingrid said, "but I am sure you saved both the doctor and me a great deal of trouble."

"Yes, I believe I did," Ives said. "Dillon is a scoundrel and Johnston is worse because he can always hire the guns of men like Metzger and Dillon. He hates Doctor Edgar more than anyone else because he has had the courage to oppose him." He looked at her gravely. "I am not proud of myself, Miss Carlson. You see, I worked for the colonel until a few minutes ago. Now I wonder why I didn't quit months ago."

"I am glad you have quit now," she said. "Won't you come in, Mr. Ives? I could fix some — " She hesitated, not sure what the right drink would be for a man like this. She said tentatively, "Some tea."

"No thank you," Ives said. "I have to get back to the hotel and pack. I am leaving town on the next stage."

He turned and stepped off the porch. This was no place for him. The memory of his wasted years rushed through his mind. With it was the mental picture of the man he should have been, the man he had once intended to be.

He heard her say, "Mr. Ives." He turned back and looked at her. She said, "The words 'Thank you' seem so terribly inadequate. Isn't there something I can do for you? Or the doctor?"

Ives smiled. She was so youthful and eager. He said, "I will be gone long before the doctor wakes up, but there is something you can do. If you know where Burns is, tell him to get help. Campbell. Scanlan. The Hallorans. Anybody. There are too many of them here in town. He is up against a coward and a killer. That is a bad combination. They are afraid of him, so they will do anything they can to destroy him."

He tipped his hat to her, a typical, gallant gesture, and walked away, leaving her staring after him, her face very pale. He was not sure whether she knew where Burns was or not. He had not asked her. It was better if he did not know. She would have been embarrassed if he had asked. Probably she would not have told him anyway.

He had done all he could and it made him feel a little less guilty. He had just about an hour to pack up. He would go to Tucson. Or maybe on west to California. He smiled, thinking of Lloyd Burns with his devil-may-care manner and Ingrid Carlson with her violet eyes and the dimples that appeared in her cheeks when she smiled.

He did not see Black Dillon standing at the rear of a building in the alley to his right. He did not hear the shot. The bullet struck him in the side of the head and killed him instantly. Dillon was gone long before anyone found the body of Calhoun Ives.

Chapter Thirty

Both Mrs. Edgar and Polly were away when Black Dillon came to the Edgar house. When Mrs. Edgar returned late in the afternoon, she brought word that Calhoun Ives had been shot to death and the murderer had escaped.

"I hate to say it but it is good riddance," Mrs. Edgar said. "Perhaps if we give them enough time Colonel Johnston's men will all destroy themselves."

Ingrid's eyes filled with tears. She wiped them away, chills running up and down her spine as she looked at Mrs. Edgar, thinking of Ives who had been alive just a short time before. She whispered, "Mr. Ives was not like the others," and told her aunt what had happened.

Mrs. Edgar's face turned pale and she sat down suddenly as if her knees could no longer hold her. She said, "I did not think that even Black Dillon would resort to violence, but he might have killed you. And Robert, too. To think that you were saved by that man Ives — "

"A good man," Ingrid interrupted fiercely.

"Of course he was," Mrs. Edgar said. "He must have been." She sighed. "At least Polly wasn't home. She would have been terribly frightened."

"Now that you are home, I am going to take a walk," Ingrid said. "I must get outside. I will start screaming if I stay here."

"I don't think you should."

"Oh, I will be all right," Ingrid said. "Dillon won't come back after what has happened."

"Don't be gone long," Mrs. Edgar worried. "I am afraid for you if you aren't afraid for yourself."

"I will be back soon," Ingrid promised.

Her steps took her back to the place along the creek where she had first met Randy Mac-Neill. She walked slowly among the cottonwoods, her eyes on the water that rushed so noisily over the rocks, tipping up and dropping over them in tiny little whitecaps. She hoped she would find Randy here, although she did not really expect to. He would be far away by now, perhaps in Three Cedars talking to his brother's partners.

Now that she thought about it, she hoped he was there. He would be safe. Calhoun Ives had been right in saying there were too many of them here in Tail Holt. Randy had told her he was going to run away to live to fight another day. And yet that did not seem like him. He was a reckless young man, too reckless for his own good. Perhaps that was one of the things she liked about him. But there was another side of it, too. Anyone who loved him would always be worried about him.

She was transfixed by surprise when she heard his voice asking, "What are you doing here?" He stood beside a cottonwood directly ahead of her. He seemed to be looking past her toward town, right hand on the butt of his gun, his head tipped to one side as if he were listening for something. Then she understood. He was considering the possibility she had been followed.

She ran to him. "No one followed me. I didn't have any idea I would find you here. I was just out walking."

He smiled at her, relaxing, his hand dropping away from gun butt. "I don't reckon you did know I was here."

"Randy, you said you were going to run away so you could fight another day. It seems to me you did not run very far."

He shook his head ruefully. "To tell the truth, I didn't much like the idea of running at all, but I figured I was in a hornet's nest. I thought they would jump to the conclusion I had headed for High Grass Valley or Three Cedars. If they did, they will be surprised when I show up tonight."

She had been happy and relieved to see him, but now she realized what he meant to do and she was not at all happy. "I suppose you are going to walk right into the Wagon Wheel and shoot a lot of men and be a big hero. Randy MacNeill, I am not going to let you do anything of the kind."

He looked at her anxiously, wondering if the dream he had dreamed so many times was all foolishness. Did the concern which she genuinely felt for him mean that she cared for him? He reached out and took her hands.

"Ingrid," he said, "every single man in Arizona who has seen you is in love with you and

251

that includes my brother Tom. I suppose most of them have asked you to marry them. Now I am going to add myself to that list. I love you. Will you . . . " He stopped. This was the last thing he had intended to say. He had no right to say it, at least not until he had finished what he must do.

"Why did you stop?" she asked breathlessly. "Did I do something wrong?"

"Oh no. But right now it is enough to say I love you. I may not be alive by morning. I suppose I am foolish to think you would marry me since you have turned down so many men, but — "

"Randy."

She tipped her head back to look into his face, knowing that it was wrong for a nice girl to let a man know she loved him until he asked her to marry him, and he had not quite asked. But he had started to, she told herself. Pride was a small thing, too small to keep her from saying what she wanted to say. Whatever happened, she could not let him go into town and be killed.

He asked, "Well?"

"Don't you know that it is not the number of men a girl turns down that counts? They are the wrong ones. She would never turn down the right one, if he ever got around to asking her."

"But he would do an awful thing if he asked her to marry him and got killed a few hours after — "

"Randy, you must not go into town. That is what I am trying to say. I didn't know how I felt about you until I saw you today and realized the terrible danger you were in. I know now. You must not let them kill you."

He said softly, "Let's sit down." He took her arm and steered her toward the creek. After they were seated on the bank, he began, "Ingrid, I — "

"Wait," she said. "There is something I must tell you first."

Perhaps he did not fully understand how far Black Dillon would go, she thought. If she told him what had happened this afternoon, he would realize that to go into town this evening would be certain death. But as she mentioned Dillon coming to the house, she saw his brown face grow darker with suppressed fury. She had only made things worse.

"Ives said to tell you there were too many of them," she cried.

"But Ives is dead," he said in a low tone. "I won't have to worry about him. Just Dillon and Colonel Johnston. The others are riffraff." He leaned toward her. "Now listen to me. I would never have forgiven myself if

253

anything had happened to you this afternoon. I would always have known I should have killed Dillon a long time ago. A rattlesnake never changes, Ingrid. That is what Dillon will be as long as he is alive."

He must not let her see that the prospect of meeting Black Dillon disturbed him. Or that he did not know how to deal with Johnston if he did succeed in killing Dillon. It would be impossible for him to kill a man who would not fight. He was certain that Johnston would crawl out of town on his belly before he would pull a gun.

She looked at him, utterly miserable. He had always been so gay and lighthearted, but now he was calm, almost stubborn, and filled with a deadly purpose. Telling him about Dillon had only strengthened his determination.

"Is there anything I can say or do that will change your mind?" she asked.

"No. A man has to do what he has to do." He rose and helped her to her feet. "It will be dark before long. You go home. I will see you after while."

For a moment she did not move, a tall and lovely girl who had told him in her way that she loved him. In the fading light here among the cottonwoods her violet eyes seemed almost black. Suddenly without a word she whirled and ran away from him. He noticed again the graceful fluent ease with which she moved. He had never seen another girl like her. He was certain there was no other.

He would see her after while, he told himself. He had to. Some men searched all their lives for their mates and never found the right ones, but he had. No one, Black Dillon or Colonel Johnston or anyone else, would keep him from going to her.

Chapter Thirty-one

An awful fear was in Colonel Johnston. Fear was an old and familiar feeling for him, but tonight it was different. He was terrified. With it was a feeling of resentment toward the people of Tail Holt who hated him. He had done a great deal for the town, but they did not know what the word gratitude meant. When he was in trouble, not one of them would come to his help except those who were on his pay roll. These were second-grade men, the ones who were left, all but Black Dillon.

Now that darkness covered the town, Johnston was afraid to leave the office in the Wagon Wheel. He sat at the desk, his hands fisted on the polished mahogany, a revolver between his hands. Ordinarily he was afraid of guns unless they were in the hands of men like Black Dillon who were both friendly and capable.

The trouble was that only Dillon survived among the men he thought he could depend upon. That was why he had taken the revolver from the desk drawer where Metzger had kept it. Lloyd Burns might get past Dillon. If he did, Johnston would use the gun.

No one, not even Butch Halloran, had kicked up the dust this young devil Burns had. To make it worse, he had fooled Johnston into hiring him and thus putting him in a position where he could spy on Johnston and his organization.

He had not thought of it before, but now it occurred to him that Burns might have been the one who had killed Hank Sowder. Certainly he had killed Dolph Metzger. In all likelihood he had shot Calhoun Ives this afternoon. Not that it made any difference. Ives had deserted Johnston, but Burns, of course, would not know that. The shooting of Ives simply proved what Johnston already knew, that the young cowboy was a vicious, hardened killer. For the first time in the years that Dillon had acted as his guard, Johnston was not sure the fellow could do the job he had been hired to do.

Whatever happened now, Johnston told himself, he had come down a long way. Black Dillon had dealt himself in as a full partner. More than that, he had secured permission to handle the men as he chose. He was too reckless. That would be their undoing. Dillon would bring the law down on their —

From outside in the alley behind the Wagon Wheel the familiar words came to Johnston's ears:

"The dirty little coward
Who shot Johnny Howard,
They have laid Jesse James in his grave."

Johnston froze. The first time he had heard that song after Tom MacNeill's killing he had been afraid of the supernatural. Now the thought did not enter his mind. It was Lloyd Burns. He must not have left Tail Holt after killing Dolph Metzger. He could not have come back, the roads guarded as they were. At least it seemed unlikely. Whether he had left or stayed in town, he had been here several hours if he had shot Calhoun Ives.

Sowder! Metzger! Ives! Johnston had no doubt he was next on Burns's list. The killer was right out there, probably not more than twenty feet from where Johnston sat. Black

Dillon was on the other side of the wall in the big gaming room, slapping people on the back and shaking hands just as Dolph Metzger had done. Suddenly Johnston remembered what Ives had told him that afternoon: "Sooner or later, Colonel, your whole empire will fall on your head."

The song started again, "The dirty little coward — " In a sudden frenzy Johnston jumped to his feet. He picked up the gun and running to the window, tore the green blind down that covered the office window facing the alley. He smashed the glass with the barrel of his gun and shoving his hand through the broken window, began firing. Once he had started he could not stop until the gun was empty.

Men rushed into the office from the game room, Dillon in the lead. Johnston pulled his arm back and leaned against the wall, trembling so he could hardly talk. Dillon shouted at him, "What happened, Colonel?"

"Burns." Johnston wiped sweat from his face. "Outside. Singing that Jesse James song."

Dillon whirled and ran out of the office, calling to the others to follow. There was a storeroom next to the office that had a door opening into the alley. Dillon would go through that door into the alley and search for

Burns until he found him and killed him.

Relieved by that thought, Johnston walked to the desk, found a box of shells for his revolver, and after ejecting the empties, reloaded. He had just finished when Dillon came back in and kicked the door shut.

"Are you drunk, Colonel?" Dillon demanded. "Or are you so scared that you are having nightmares?"

So he had not found Burns after all! Johnston said angrily, "I will not listen to your insolence — "

"Burns wasn't out there. I could not even find any tracks in the dust. I don't believe he is in town. I think he went after the Hallorans and we will not see them until sometime tomorrow."

"We are goners if he brings those scoundrels to town," Johnston said in a low voice: "We do not have enough men — "

"We have enough if we use them right," Dillon broke in impatiently. "That was a fool idea you had about guarding the roads. We have scattered our men so we don't have any strength anywhere."

"It was not just my idea," Johnston defended himself. "You said you intended doing it."

"I did not say that," Dillon differed. "I would never have done a thing as stupid as

259

that. If it wasn't far to High Grass Valley we would have a fight on our hands tonight. You can be damned sure I will call the boys in tomorrow morning."

Johnston looked at Dillon sharply. He was used to the man's arrogance. No amount of reprimanding cured him. But this was different. He was lying about it not being his idea to send the men out to guard the roads. Johnston distinctly remembered making the suggestion and hearing Dillon say that was what he intended to do.

Dillon must have some purpose, Johnston thought wildly. Then he guessed what it was, and the thought sent a chill down his spine. Dillon aimed to kill him. Now that he was a full partner, Dillon would receive everything if Johnston died. It would be a simple matter for the guard to murder him and lay it onto Burns.

Johnston did not let Dillon suspect that he knew. He said, "I am going home." He slipped the gun inside his waistband. "You can see that everything is in shape before you leave."

"You are afraid to go home in the dark," Dillon sneered. "A booger will get you. A booger named Lloyd Burns."

Johnston did not say anything. He walked out of the office and across the big gaming room to the batwing doors. He did not understand his own feelings, but he was no longer afraid. For years he had hired men and hidden behind them. Now they were all gone except Black Dillon who aimed to kill him. He was as certain of that as he was certain that Burns was after him.

He was not aware that Dillon was behind him until he was outside the Wagon Wheel. He did not want the guard to go with him. He had to go home and lock the doors and try to decide what to do. He said in a trembling voice, "You stay here."

"If Burns is in town, I had better go with you," Dillon said. "I will come back. You will be safe in the house if you lock the doors, although I do not think he is within ten miles of here."

Johnston was not sure whether Dillon was rawhiding him or not. If the guard insisted on going with him there was nothing he could do. When they were in the darkness, the lights of the business block behind them, Johnston lifted the gun from his waistband and put it into his right hand pocket. Dillon was not a smart man. He was so foolish that he thought he could manage all of Johnston's enterprises, but he would be broke in six months.

The truth was that it had taken a combination of Johnston's brains and Dillon's ruthless disregard for life to be successful. Johnston smiled in the darkness as they turned up the walk to their house. He had a strange feeling, as if he had been changed into a different man. He would turn Dillon's idea around. If he killed the guard, everyone would think it was Burns. It was the only thing he could do. Dillon was going to kill him if he didn't get the gunman first.

They went into the house, Johnston remaining by the door while Dillon went across the room to light a lamp. Johnston's right hand was in his coat pocket wrapped around the butt of his gun. He was astonished at his coolness. He knew exactly what he had to do. There would be no risk, for this was the last thing Dillon would expect.

Johnston would get out of town. When he returned he would bring men with him, good men he could depend on. Then he would go after the Hallorans. They had been a threat too long. Burns was his only worry. Somehow he had to dodge him until he was able to leave town.

Dillon lighted the lamp and slipped the chimney into place. When he turned, he said, "I will take a look through the house — "

He stopped, his eyes on Johnston's face that held a puzzling expression. Dillon had never seen him look this way before. Johnston raised his left hand to his forehead and held it there. He stood like that, his eyes as wild as those of a forest animal.

"You intended to kill me and lay it to Burns," Johnston said. "That was why you made me draw up that partnership agreement. It won't work, Black."

"No, you fool — " Dillon yelled.

Johnston fired twice, tongues of flame leaping through the cloth of his coat. Even at this short distance, he missed both shots. Dillon drew his gun and before Johnston could fire a third time, the guard shot him through the heart.

For a long time Dillon stared down at the dead banker, completely puzzled. Johnston must have gone loco, he thought. He had lived with his fears too long. Dillon shook his head, his eyes still on the dead man. "You should not have done it, Colonel," he said aloud. "We needed each other."

Chapter Thirty-two

Randy stood in the weeds of the vacant lot across the alley from the rear of the Wagon Wheel when he sang the Jesse James song. He was familiar enough with Johnston's habits to be reasonably sure he was in the office, now that Metzger was dead.

The instant Johnston tore the blind down and knocked the glass out of the window, Randy slipped back across the vacant lot to the side street where he had left his horse. He mounted and rode toward Johnston's house, convinced that tonight was the time to end this.

Randy's sole purpose in using the Jesse James song had been to work on Johnston's fears until he broke. Judging by the way he smashed the window glass and fired wildly into the night, he was close to breaking now.

The only question in Randy's mind was what the banker would do next. He might stay in the Wagon Wheel where Black Dillon could guard him. Dillon would probably re-

264

main there until closing time. Somebody had to run the place. With Metzger and Ives gone, Dillon was the only one left to take over.

Half a block from Johnston's house Randy drew up and dismounted, still wondering what the banker would do. If the tinhorn Walker had taken word to Johnston that Randy was going to bring Tom MacNeill's partners as well as the Halloran gang to Tail Holt, the colonel would not stay in the Wagon Wheel. He would want no part of the fight that was certain to follow.

Johnston should know that this could not happen tonight. The distance was so great to Three Cedars and High Grass Valley that it would be impossible for Randy to reach both places and get back to Tail Holt so soon. Remembering how Johnston had dived in panic behind the piano the night the Hallorans had dropped into the Wagon Wheel, Randy was certain that he would be incapable of doing any calm reasoning about when the Hallorans and the Argonaut men would arrive.

Randy cautiously approached the Johnston house, staying on the opposite side of the street. He was prepared to wait, for Johnston would certainly come home sooner or later. He was surprised that he had to wait only a very short time.

The night was so dark that Randy could not

see who was going into the house until the lamp was lighted. He crossed the street and stopped in the gate, hearing the talk between Johnston and Dillon. Through the open door he saw the shooting.

Randy took two long steps through the gate. He lifted his gun out of the holster and eased it back, then he called, "Dillon."

The gunman spun around and stared into the darkness. He made a perfect target standing with the lighted lamp behind him. If his and Randy's position had been reversed, he would have fired, but Randy was not a man who could take advantage of such a situation. Dillon knew that, so he did not move.

The gunman called in a hard bitter voice, "You can't cut the mustard this time, Burns. Come on into the light and take your medicine."

"One of us will take it," Randy said. "Before the fireworks start, I want you to know that Tom MacNeill was my brother."

If the news shocked Dillon he did not show it. He said harshly, "Tom MacNeill got what he deserved. So will you. If it wasn't for you, the colonel would not have tried to kill me. You got him so scared he did not know what he was doing. I told you before you were too biggity for a two-spot in the deck. No wet-eared kid can take Black Dillon. Come on. Show yourself."

Still Randy stood outside the finger of light falling past Dillon. For a long time he had worried about facing this killer, but now to his surprise he found he was not worried at all. He had reached the end of a long trail. He said quietly, "You are afraid, Black. You're hiding behind your tough talk."

Dillon stepped forward, cursing as he came down off the porch. "You ain't such a hell-popper. You're the one that's yellow or you wouldn't hide in the dark."

Randy moved forward, right hand just above his gun butt, his body balanced forward on the balls of his feet. He said, "You can see me now, Dillon."

Still cursing, Dillon drew his gun. He threw a shot that was a complete miss. Randy did not try to match Dillon's speed because he knew he could not, but he did fire before Dillon could get off a second shot. He did not miss. It was this deliberate coolness that saved his life.

Dillon was knocked back against the porch railing. He squeezed the trigger, the bullet kicking up dust in the street behind Randy. He held himself upright, his feet braced in front of him. He started to bring his gun level again when Randy fired a second time. Dillon's knees folded and he collapsed, his arms flung out.

For a moment Randy did not move, his smoking gun in his hand. Suddenly he was aware that men were moving around him. They slapped him on the back and shook his hand and announced that it was a good night's work, that nobody was going to shed any tears over Black Dillon's demise. Or Colonel Johnston's, either.

Doctor Edgar appeared with his black bag in his hand as he always did when he heard shooting. He shook his head, first over Dillon and then over Colonel Johnston, and said there was nothing he could do for them. Randy escaped from the crowd and walked beside Doctor Edgar, leading his horse.

"There's one thing I don't savvy," Randy said, and told the doctor about the manner in which Johnston had died. "He actually tried to kill Dillon," Randy finished. "He must have gone crazy."

"I think it is probable that is exactly what happened," Doctor Edgar said thoughtfully. "Perhaps he had been crazy to some extent for a long time. His passion for power and money would indicate that. He was at least a strange man. He liked to appear pious and gave liberally to the church. Such behavior does not make sense when you place it alongside the crimes we know he ordered his hired ruffians to commit."

"I still don't savvy," Randy said.

"What I am trying to say is that the lives of most men are reasonably predictable," the doctor said. "Johnston's was not. He was a coward and perhaps he hated himself for it. I judge that his sanity hung by a thin thread. Something may have broken that thread. The deaths of Metzger and Ives, for instance. After that he was afraid even of Black Dillon."

It might have been the deaths of Metzger and Ives, Randy reflected. Or the Jesse James song. Then he thought of Dillon who had been a better man with a gun than he was, but the guard's fury and hate had more than balanced that advantage, so he had hurried his shot and had died.

"Our troubles are over," the doctor said. "Your brother can safely come back from Tucson. Scanlan and Campbell can work their mine without interference. I am convinced that the Halloran gang will break up because there is no need for Butch to hold them together. And certainly the scoundrels who were on Johnston's pay roll will leave the country. And now what are your plans, sir?"

"I figured on staying here and throwing in with Tom and his partners," Randy said. "Do you think that Ingrid — "

His voice trailed off. He could not find the

right words to say what was in his mind. The doctor laughed softly. "I think she will. Now it is up to you."

Ahead of them the lights in the doctor's house were inviting him. Behind the windows Ingrid would be waiting. He was sick of guns and bloodshed. He wanted to hold the girl he loved in his arms. He wanted to be with Tom and to work in peace. He wanted a home and a family — He hurried toward the beckoning windows. There were so many things to tell Ingrid.

THORNDIKE PRESS hopes you have enjoyed this Large Print book. All our Large Print titles are designed for easy reading, and all our books are made to last. Other Thorndike Press books are available at your library, through selected bookstores, or directly from the publisher. For more information about current and upcoming titles, please call or mail your name and address to:

THORNDIKE PRESS
PO Box 159
Thorndike, Maine 04986
800/223-6121
207/948-2962